A

CANDLELIGHT ECSTASY ROMANCE

Candlelight Ecstasy Romances

The Passionate Touch

Bonnie Drake

A Candlelight Ecstasy Romance

Published by
Dell Publishing Co., Inc.
1 Dag Hammarskjold Plaza
New York, New York 10017

Dell ® TM 681510, Dell Publishing Co., Inc.

ISBN: 0-440-16776-0

Printed in the United States of America

First printing—January 1981

The
Passionate
Touch

CHAPTER 1

The bright midmorning sun obligingly poked its golden
head from behind the schools of scurrying clouds just
as Eva Jordenson lifted the camera to her eye. It had
been the first time she had done so since she had left
New York the previous evening. In fact, although her
camera had been her ever-present, ever-faithful companion of the last few years, she had been unusually
neglectful of it during the ordeal of the last month. It
had been in the middle of a particularly difficult and
challenging assignment that she had received the news
of her husband's illness. She had dropped everything
to be with him.

The taste of bitterness was strong in her mouth as
she let her mind wander back. Yes, she had dropped
everything to be with him, as she had always done during their brief three years of marriage. It had begun as
infatuation; she had met Stu while she was at college
and had immediately fallen for his breathtaking good
looks, his undeniable charm as a ladies' man, and his
apparent success in the business, owned by his family,
which he had entered directly from business school and

had managed to turn into a multimillion-dollar enterprise within a few short years. Stu had swept Eva off her feet, both figuratively and literally, and she had remained thus until the shattering day when she first realized that it had always been, and would continue to be, Stu's habit of sweeping attractive young women off their feet.

Now, as she gazed through the view finder at her surroundings in this small airport in Belo Horizonte, she wondered if Brazil would take her far enough away from the multitude of emotions she had suffered with these past weeks. Would she ever be able to shed the mantle of guilt that threatened to dominate her future for years to come? She had badly needed to get away, to escape the overpowering atmosphere of mourning which had filled each day since Stu's death. But was she strong enough to free her mind from its burden, as she had done to her body by boldly ignoring the indignant protests of her late husband's family and making use of the reservation which Stu had originally made for himself aboard the Pan Am jet to Rio de Janeiro?

The flight from Kennedy had been long, though uneventful. Upon her arrival at Rio's Galeão Airport, Eva had risked life and limb by taking a taxi across town. Never again would she voice one word of complaint about New York taxi drivers; the harrowing ride here in Rio, seemingly run-of-the-mill from the looks of the other drivers on th road, had certainly diverted Eva's mind from her private battle for a few minutes. It was with a weak though heartfelt sigh of relief that Eva had stepped safely from the taxi at Santos Dumont Airport, knowing that no amount of fear of flying could equal the tension in the brief ride she had just taken.

Once she had boarded the Trans-Brasil plane, it had

been a comfortable shuttle from Rio to Belo. A full-course meal had been graciously served, along with a glass of native Brazilian wine, which, to Eva's mildly though by no means expertly trained palate, was as rich-bodied as any she had tasted. The wine had begun to dull her senses when she was brought gently back to earth by the *cafèzinho* which had topped off the menu. Never before an admirer of espresso of any form, Eva had found much enjoyment in this rich, sweet, very strong black coffee.

Thus, she had emerged from the plane at Belo in a most composed manner, one which continued to grace her as she put in her request at the appropriate desk for a driver to take her on the last leg of her journey. It had only been during the leisure moments, as she waited with her traveling bags and camera equipment at her feet, that her mind had begun to sink into the quicksand again. With as much determination as she could muster, Eva forced herself into serious contemplation of the sights around her. Many of the other passengers who had disembarked with her had already left the terminal. Of the others who remained, she found herself gazing at a diverse gathering of people, most of whom seemed completely at home, relaxed, and satisfied as they awaited their own contacts. She released the shutter several times, advancing the film to the first frames, and was grateful for the hum of the ongoing conversations which would effectively cover up her photographic activity. No one gave the slightest sign of objection to, much less recognition of, the camera before her. She photographed a group of children who were seated with a stunningly attractive *mameluco* woman, her proud Indian features blended exquisitely with the white pallor of her smooth skin. Each of the children would have made a portrait by and of himself;

each child varied in skin tone, hair color, and clothing from his companions, yet each seemed as contented, as loved, as the next.

Eva shifted her sights to the building itself, extending her zoom lens to capture the architecture of this building which, like so much of the city around it, was relatively young and indicative of the prosperity which had come to this region of Brazil as a result of its vast mining interests. She photographed the small, well-stocked, open-fronted airport shops carrying their wide sampling of Brazilian goods. The attractive rows of silver, pewter, and leather goods would certainly add a flavor to her photojournalistic effort, as would the stalls of hand-loomed tablecloths, bedspreads, and straw goods.

As the camera's eye led her back into the central terminal waiting room, her view swept past, then promptly backtracked to focus on two individuals, a man and a woman, who were deeply engaged in a conversation by the airline desk. The woman, obviously an airline employee in her crisply tailored, properly insigniaed navy suit, presented a striking image of sophistication and confidence, her blond hair pulled back into a knot at the nape of her neck, serving to further emphasize her beautifully made-up features, laid open for the world to savor. For Eva, however, the major focus was elsewhere, as she zoomed in on the figure next to the stewardess. It was male from head to foot, more male than Eva had ever been aware existed. Standing at his full height momentarily as he shifted position to more intimately converse with his companion, he reached to well over six feet. His thick head full of casually groomed black hair showed the slightest, and most dashing, hint of gray at the sideburns, adding several years to his overall appearance, which was that of a man in his mid-thirties. His skin, tautly drawn over high cheekbones, bore evidence of a life under the sun, though whether in business or in pleasure Eva had no way of knowing. His dress was as casual as his features —lightweight, tan trousers molding to his lean legs and thighs, a cream-colored shirt, open at the neck to reveal short tufts of black hair on a chest which, from the firm lines emerging suggestively through the thin fabric, promised to be as broad and strong as any woman might wish it. His jacket, a matching tan to the pants, and tie were nonchalantly draped over one arm, which in turn was draped around the stewardess; his other arm rested in a relaxed manner on the high desk next to him. The overall picture, as Eva preserved it in her mind—for she found herself totally unable to function as a photographer with this man in her sights—was one of masculinity, strength, and sureness, peppered with the barest hint of arrogance which a particular tilt of the chin can betray.

Subconsciously, Eva had held her breath as her eyes remained frozen on this stranger. Now she slowly exhaled as her total impression merged into one powerful image. Then, slowly and silently, that one powerful image raised his dark eyes from those of his companion and turned them toward Eva. Through no conscious decision on her part, Eva, who had been observing this compelling figure entirely through her view finder, lowered her camera and allowed her green eyes to meet his challenging gaze, which, in a split second's time and with barely a flicker, widened to take in the whole of her. As if in retribution for her previous examination of him, of which she was positive he had been unaware, his eyes scrutinized her seated form, intimately examining her shoulder-length curly hair, its brown sheen sparkling wtih red highlights as the sun hit it through the skylight above, and her graceful neck and straight shoulders, whose span was broken only by the spaghetti straps of the sun dress, which she had so wisely changed into at the airport in Rio, having arrived from New York in warmer clothes more appropriate to the month of January in the Northern Hemisphere. So penetrating was his continued gaze that Eva became thankful that her sundress was loose-fitting, leaving the only evidence of her near-perfect figure to be her shapely legs, pale as they were compared to those of the few women seated nearby. His gaze had awakened something totally strange within Eva, something of which she was only beginning to become aware when she was jolted out of this most disturbing visual interchange by a firm tap on her shoulder.

"Jordenson?" inquired a short, rotund man.

"Yes!" Eva responded with a jump, feeling her cheeks flush as she pivoted her head toward the thickly accented voice which addressed her.

"Taxi?"

With an affirmative smile, Eva quickly stood up and shifted both her pocketbook and her camera onto one shoulder as she motioned with her hand toward the bags which the driver simultaneously had spotted and was already lifting. Looking back, she checked to make sure that nothing had been left before turning to follow the driver to his taxi. It was only at the door that she paused to look at where the oddly unsettling man had been standing. There was trace neither of him nor his female admirer, which Eva was sure this woman must be. No doubt they were on their way to some intimate café, mused Eva, as she made a rational attempt to dispel the germ of discomfort this man's gaze had sent her way.

As the taxi began its journey, Eva settled into the back seat by the window, determined to view, if only in passing, this city, whose beauty and modernity would contrast greatly with the beauty and antiquity of the towns that she would be seeing shortly. With a professional ease, her camera captured many of the sights, new structures and old, graciously planted and cultivated gardens, inviting parks and plazas bounded by tree-lined avenues. Then, as the city was left behind and the highway stretched ahead, Eva permitted herself to sit back and relax. So much had happened to her life in the past few weeks. Had she been told last month that she was soon to be a widow—no less chasing some precious gem in South America—she would have laughed hysterically. Now she could laugh just as hysterically at the reality of the situation. Actually, it was Stu who had planned the trip to Brazil, a trip to be taken for pure enjoyment and, perhaps, a little enlightenment, though, Eva had pondered cynically at the time, with Stu it was always precious little of the latter and a whole lot of the former. And, as if in confirmation of this fact, Eva had not been invited. Stu had claimed, upon her objection, that the hills of central Brazil were no place for a woman. She had heard the same argument time and time again during the past three years, only to learn that what Stu had really meant was that his adventures had no place for "this" woman. It was, in fact, this repeated sentiment that had prompted Eva to go into photography. She had always been a fairly strong, capable person, and she felt stifled by the confines that Stu had established soon after their marriage. Although she was not accustomed to the kind of wealth Stu possessed, she found no inherent satisfaction in taking it for granted. She had been brought up under the old work ethic, and, even though her family had lived well, both her parents had worked, and she had done so too whenever possible during vacations and the summer. They all enjoyed working she had learned to derive satisfaction out of doing something well, be it in school or at work. Thus, when it became clear that Stu had envisioned a wife who would conform to the image of a wealthy socialite, she had balked. Photography was something she had taken to naturally. Studying it seriously was merely an extension of the fun she had had as a youngster playing with the camera her parents had given her on her birthday. When she had landed a job on the staff of a small but influential newspaper in upstate New York—where their country house had been built soon after their marriage—Eva had felt not only pride but a sense of accomplishment and a desperate hope that her job would bring some concrete direction into her life once again.

It had done just that. At the end, it was her major life line to reality. Her marriage was in shambles; she and Stu shared all of the surface trappings of a marriage with none of the sturdy fiber of love to bolster it. Although she had remained faithful to him quite willingly, he had felt none of the same type of loyalty and had made no attempt to hide it. Eva had merely looked the other way, knowing that there was very little she would have been able to do had she tried. But what if she had tried? The same old guilt feeling was always there, taunting her, punishing her, blaming her for her failure to satisfy Stu.

As the converted VW taxi approached a small town built into the hills through which they would be increasingly passing, Eva reached for her camera, motioned the driver to pull over, and climbed out of the car to take photographs from the roadside. She had found the landscape gaining in excitement as they drove. The road had begun to wind in and out of hills, each turn with its own surprises. Here the earth had taken on the iron-red color typical of this mineral-rich land. Lime-washed cottages, each with its tin-fluted roof, dotted the hillside in small clusters, the bottom-most almost reaching the bank of the narrow river, which snaked its own way through the hills. Satisfied that she had exhausted the photographic possibilities from this position, she re-entered the taxi, and it made its way once again, moving further into the less-populated regions of central Brazil.

She had to laugh to herself. A goose chase. That's what she had told Stu this trip would be. A wild-goose chase into some Godforsaken hills in search of a stone that the world neither needed nor would appreciate. The fabled Espinhaço Topaz, he had called it; it was supposedly one of the largest crystals of precious sherry-yellow topaz ever discovered. Yet it had not been seen since its discovery over one hundred and fifty years ago. Now, a Brazilian adventurer had come up with a map that was to lead to the Topaz. Only once had Stu met this Brazilian, and brief as this introduction was, Stu had committed himself to the expedition.

At the time Stu had told Eva of his proposed trip, the whole thing had sounded preposterous. Then, in the week following Stu's death and funeral, the walls had begun to close in on her to such an extent that she knew she had to get away from the entire scene. Here were the plane ticket, the instructions for reaching the small town of Terra Vermelho (the base for the search), and the letter from this Brazilian, Roberto de Carvalho, who would be leading the small group—all these things were at Eva's fingertips. The lure was too great. Eva once again yielded to the impulsiveness that, as in the case of her marriage to Stu, occasionally proved to be her one personality flaw. She discarded the somber clothes of mourning, which ill fitted both her vivacious features and her most honest inner feelings, packed her bags for a trip to the warmth of the semitropical uplands, and boarded her plane without a second thought.

Now, as the taxi moved northward, Eva was convinced that the impulse to come had been a good one. The bracing mountain air, warm though it was, seemed to be clearing her head somewhat. She began to feel her nerve endings uncoiling from the dangerous tautness which had characterized them for the past few weeks. She began to relax; a sense of well-being, as deceptive as she knew it could be, had settled on her. Wild-goose chase or not, she was determined to enjoy herself, just as Stu would have done. And yes, this trip would also be enlightening, if only from the viewpoint of the pictures she would be able to bring back for publication.

Most important, Eva was counting on this trip to put things back into perspective for her. Her disastrous marriage to Stu had temporarily sidetracked her from the kind of life she had always wanted, one that was filled with stimulation, achievement, and love.

Eva had grown up with more love than most children. Her parents were totally devoted, deeply loving, and, in their own way, overly indulgent of her. When it became obvious that she would be their only child, they even exaggerated these qualities, as a way to vent their own needs to give and to compensate for their inability to provide siblings for Eva. Far fom being overprotective, Eva's parents had given her much free rein, knowing that she would have to cope if anything ever happened to them and she was left alone in the world. Eerily, their premonition was well founded. Eva's mother became ill and died within six months of Eva's graduation from high school, and a year later, when Eva was in her first year of college, her father suffered a stroke and, after three months in a comatose condition, he too died.

Her parents' training served her well. Distraught as she was at the loss of both parents within such a short time, Eva managed to fill her days at the university, not slowing down at all until she sensed that the pain had begun to ease.

It was during her sophomore year that she met E. Stuart Jordenson. She was taking part in a work-study program which, though she had been adequately provided for by her parents, gave her both the extra money and the additional work experience that she knew would be of great benefit after she graduated. As a very part-time assistant to the editor of the in-house publication at Jordenson Manufacturing, she was given a wide assortment of chores, doing a little reporting, a little photography, a little design, a little layout. It was during one of these assignments that she had been singled out by the boss himself. How ironic, she thought now in hindsight, that this job, which she had taken specifically to improve her future prospects, had actually affected them so completely!

Stu had entered Eva's life at a time when she was uncharacteristically vulnerable, still suffering from the emotional withdrawal following her parents' deaths. He promised her everything she thought she wanted, and after a whirlwind courtship, they were married in an elaborately staged wedding attended by all of the Jordenson relatives, all of the Jordenson friends, all of the Jordenson business associates, most of the Jordenson acquaintances, and a few of Eva's close friends. Viewing Eva as a poor, unsophisticated, though perhaps devious, orphan, Stu's parents had magnanimously made all the plans for this extravaganza, relegating Eva to the role of spectator, a role she was not used to playing. The wedding preparations themselves became a nightmare of fittings, consultations, and other command performances, ironically a harbinger of the agonizing marriage yet to come.

Eva frequently asked herself, after the first few months of happiness had dragged into months of tension, frustration, and anger, why Stu had wanted to marry her in the first place. He was older, wise to the ways of women and the world, and could have—usually did have—his choice of any woman for his bedmate. Perhaps it was because Eva had resisted his advances, insisting that she would not become his lover until after she became his wife. Perhaps it was her innocence, which may have lent a freshness and sense of vitality to his overly sophisticated, boringly chic circle. Perhaps it was a pathetic attempt at rebellion against the parents who had dominated his personal life for too many years and had made it clear from the start that Eva was, in her youth, naiveté, and lack of social position, an unfit partner for their son.

Whatever the reason, Eva knew beyond a doubt that she had failed miserably to meet the challenge. Further, she realized very quickly that her failure had little to do with ability but much to do with desire. It had been a two-way street; just as Stuart Jordenson had become disillusioned with her, she had become disillusioned with him. The one thing she so badly craved, particularly following the deaths of her parents, was love; it was the one thing Stu was completely unable and unwilling to give her. As the months passed and her hurt deepened, she turned away from him even on the rare occasions when he approached her, thus compounding the ill feeling each harbored within.

If only she had tried harder. If only she had given more. If only she had demanded less. If only she had been able to convince Stu to slow down. But, as if to purposely contradict her presence, he had worked harder, played harder, even rested harder. A heart attack at the age of thirty-eight was not unheard of, but it was unusual. Eva sensed that in her heart she would blame herself for a long time to come, long after her mind became convinced of her innocence.

Eva was brought abruptly back to the present by a sudden command from the driver. His English was quite good on the phrases commonly used in his line of work, but it deteriorated rapidly with any variation from the norm. He was diligent in telling her the names of the towns they passed—Curvelo, Corinto, Buenopolis—and even attempted to tell her a little about each, most of which she had been unable to understand. This command, however, was in Portuguese, so she had no chance at all. His meaning soon became crystal clear, however, as the taxi negotiated the first of a series of hairpin turns, and Eva, belongings and all, ricocheted to the opposite door, which she held on to for dear life.

As quickly as the stomach-wrenching, 180-degree turns had begun, they were left behind as the car proceeded to pass across the gold-flecked moorland. The road gradually gained altitude as they progressed northward, and although the air here was drier than that of Rio, or even of Belo Horizonte, Eva could feel the heat increasing.

Aside from the charm of the towns, each tucked into its own niche on its own hillside, the landscape itself drew Eva's attention. With her window rolled down to allow more air into the already warm taxi, she photographed the long grasses as they swayed with the breeze, blowing first one way and then the other, creating bold patterns on the surface of the upland plain. As the road gracefully undulated its way through another mountainous pass, she photographed the razor-sharp outline of the purple rocks silhouetted by the sun. A further turn of the road revealed a peaceful cluster of woodland growth whose trees were foliated with as great a variety as there was said to be among the Brazilians themselves. Many of the trees were flowered; Eva's film would capture the golden yellow flowers of one, the mauve of another, the blue of yet another, before she placed the camera on the seat beside her and let her own eye take its turn to admire this natural beauty. Yes, it was beautiful, she had to concede. Her preconception of this country had been so wrong; no land which spawned such natural wealth, as rugged as it was at some points, could ever be called "Godforsaken."

Since it left Belo Horizonte the taxi was able to move steadily ahead, unencumbered by the traffic that had bogged it down in the city. Eva was aware of other automobiles as they progressed northward, but each kept its pace consistent with the terrain. Occasionally, and of greater interest to Eva, the taxi passed men and donkeys. These men, often short of height and swarthy of complexion, were dressed in the light-colored, loose-fitting work clothes so appropriate to the climate. Each pair of feet was protected from the roughness underfoot by heavy-duty work shoes, seemingly held together after years of use by red-tinted mud and layers of dust that caked the seams. Each head was crowned with the obligatory hat, unstructured, wide-brimmed, and well worn, providing a token measure of privacy from the elements, both human and natural.

It appeared to Eva that these particular Brazilians, leading their heavily burdened donkeys from one rural area to another, were shy people who felt totally content within their own millieu but might resent the intrusion of an outsider in their daily lives.

Strange, she thought, the extremes she had seen in her first few hours in this country—these wayside travelers, exuding a purely natural, rugged, uncultivated kind of raw beauty as compared with the refined air of sophistication and studied perfection of the city dwellers. For the first time since leaving the airport at Belo several hours ago, Eva recalled the man she had seen there whose gaze then had sent such disturbing currents from one end of her body to the other. A sixth sense told her that his beauty was as genuine as that of his more bedraggled countrymen. Yet she felt her guard rising, even as she mentally re-evaluated him. This man, she told herself, probably had more in common wth her late husband and his circle of friends and admirers than either had with these simple country workers. She had learned the hard way about this type of man. He used people for his own ends, playing one against the other as it suited him, taking everything he could get until there was either nothing left to take or someone else whose givings were more promising. Eva knew that the power this man must have over women, so clearly conveyed to her in his earlier scrutiny of her and her own reaction to it, could prove devastating to the woman who should let herself become ensnared.

No, Eva was determined that she would never let herself be hurt again by such a man. The wound was still raw from her marriage to Stu; she must let its dull ache be a steady reminder, a repeated warning against any who would prey on her vulnerability. But then, this expedition had physically removed her from the rat race; she need have no fear of any scheming playboys in Terra Vermelho.

Terra Vermelho. No sooner had her thoughts formed than the words were echoed by her driver. Indeed, as she gazed to the right she caught her first glimpse of the town as it silently emerged from the late afternoon mist that had so protectively concealed it from the outside world.

CHAPTER 2

The taxi made a sharp turn off the main highway onto a narrow asphalt road that threaded its way carefully between alternating rock formations and low woodland patches. The descent into this mountainside pocket was a gradual one, enabling Eva to leisurely view, both by eye and through her camera lens, the town which lay directly below. With mountains looming all around, the town had been solidly built on the graduated steps at the base of one of the gentler inclines. The houses were set in clusters, some at the lowest levels of the pocket, some a short way up the hillside, with a wide smattering on the middle tiers. The buildings themselves were of a natural gray limestone, varying in shades from the freshest off-white to the more weathered tones. Most were of a single story; a very few were graced with a second floor. All were designed with the tall, narrow doors and windows trimmed in blue in the style so typical of the Portuguese who had originally settled the area. The roofs were constructed of red tiles, faded to a shade compatible with the earth-red hue of the roadside. Clumps of low growing trees and shrubbery dotted the layout, with an occasional palm frond jutting up in cowlick fashion around the corner of a house, as a reminder to the inhabitants that nature would always have the final say.

The gently flowing river, which formed a narrow ribbon winding through the town, was further testimony of this priority of nature. Those houses near the water's edge were set in postures of respect for the natural curves the river had maintained for centuries.

As the taxi entered the town, Eva fully comprehended the value of the donkeys she had seen earlier. The cobblestoned streets were by no means conducive to automotive comfort. Although she saw cars on every street, Eva supposed they must be reserved for trips to the "outside world"; certainly a bout on the back a donkey would be preferable to the discomfort to one of driving repeatedly over these roads.

The taxi came to an abrupt stop in front of one of the double-tiered structures. Eva saw no sign indicating that this was a hotel, nor did she see any increase in activity here to suggest it. Questioning, she leaned forward in her seat toward her guide.

"Is this the hotel?" she asked, her tone one of incredulity.

"Não sei. I don't know. But I leave people before. No other place I know."

His broken English and the puzzled look on his own face was indication enough to Eva that he could help her no further. Suddenly anxious to escape the warmth of the taxi and stretch her legs, she counted out and handed him the fee that the service at the airport had quoted her, adding a few more *cruzeiros* as a way of thanking him for his pleasantness and his well-intentioned attempts at playing the tour guide. Stepping out of the taxi, she gingerly straightened her legs as she ran her hands up and down the back muscles which had become stiff from inactivity and the mild abuse which the final stage of the journey had inflicted. In that brief instant, Eva felt besieged by the fatigue she had successfully warded off earlier, increasing her determination to settle into a hotel room as soon as possible.

As the taxi backed into a side street, turned, and headed in the direction it had come, Eva bent to pick up her large suitcase, smaller cosmetic case, and duffel bag which, containing the camera equipment, was by far the heaviest. The air was warmer than she had anticipated, and beads of sweat formed on her forehead and upper lip as she struggled rather clumsily toward the open door of what she assumed, for lack of any better choice, to be the hotel. Had the street not been practically deserted she would have stopped someone for directions. As it was, the few people she did see were a slight distance away and Eva supposed, quite correctly it later turned out, that she would have trouble making herself understood to these very native Brazilians.

The heat of the afternoon sun abated as Eva passed through the entrance of this house and found herself in a large, high-ceilinged living room sparsely furnished with a pair of chairs and a low bench of highly polished jacaranda, a rosewood native to Brazil, and an intricately designed hammock, stretched from wall to wall at one corner of the room. A low wooden table, simple but solidly designed and of the same gleaming dark wood as the chairs, stood slightly off center in the room, and beneath it, the one source of vibrant color in the room, was a handsome red and gold-flecked rug, hand woven in a pattern typical of the Indian tribes of the Amazon basin.

Eva put down her bags to examine the room. It suddenly occurred to her that this did not appear to be a hotel at all but rather someone's private residence, into which she was a possibly unwelcome intruder. Despite the open door and windows, there was no sign of anyone nearby. Cautiously, Eva took a further step into the room, leaving her bags by the door where she had originally deposited them.

"Hello?" Eva paused, reluctant to disturb the privacy of this house any more than was absolutely necessary.

"Hello?" she began timidly, though a little louder than before. "Is anybody here? . . . Hello!"

Her voice had progressively increased in volume and her final shout must have reached its mark, for she soon heard the sound of scurrying footsteps approaching from the rear of the house. As their patter grew louder, Eva turned expectantly toward a doorway on her left just in time to see a rolypoly little woman sweep into the room. The smooth flow of her full skirt halted immediately, fold bumping into fold before falling back into place, when the pleasant, round face spotted Eva. Immediately, Eva was engulfed by a flood of words of the guttural Portuguese so foreign to her. An excellent student of languages in school, her training had been in Latin and French, neither of which now sounded remotely similar to these words which were bombarding her at breakneck speed.

Eva held both hands up in front of her, open palms patting the air, gesturing her hostess to slow down.

"I can't understand you. Do you speak any English?"

The suddenly blank expression on the woman's hitherto expressive face was answer enough to Eva's query.

"Hotel?" Eva tried once more, now accompanying her words with primitive sign language, first pointing to her bags, then washing her face with imaginary water, finally closing her eyes and resting her head on her palm-to-palm hands. For at this point the exhaustion of her long journey—it had been almost twenty-four hours since she had left the New York town house she and Stu had shared—had begun to take its toll, and as pleased as Eva was to have reached her destination on schedule, she was anxious to get some rest before she was to rendezvous with the others in the expedition.

Eva's attempts at communicating faltered briefly as she realized with a gasp that she had no idea where the rendezvous was to occur. She had taken for granted that this small town would have but one hotel, where she would immediately be able to contact other members of the group. If she couldn't communicate with someone soon, she would have to spend the rest of the day searching for these headquarters by trial and error. And in her present physical condition, she dreaded that prospect.

Reaching into her pocketbook, she drew out the letter that was tucked neatly beside her passport and return airline ticket. As she opened it and scanned its contents, which she had read thoroughly several times before leaving New York, she was reminded that the group was to gather at eight that evening. But there was no address given, no location suggested for this meeting. Eva swore silently to herself; her first major miscalculation—this information must have been conveyed to Stu verbally by this Roberto de Carvalho. And in the wake of her hasty decision to go to Brazil in place of Stu, Eva had failed to notify this man either of her husband's death or of her intention of substituting for him.

Her attention returned to the woman in whose house she was so unceremoniously getting nowhere.

"Roberto de Carvalho? Do you know him? I must contact Roberto de Carvalho." The words were spoken very slowly, as if careful enunciation would bridge the language barrier.

"Ah!" A broad smile spread across the woman's face, rekindling the light that had dimmed temporarily at the earlier moment's impasse. Drawing Eva to the door gently, she pointed to a house not far up the street, implying with a nod that Eva would have success there in locating this man.

Eva returned the smile with a natural warmth, grateful for the woman's patience. Reaching down to lift her bags once more, she was halted by a firm hand on the arm and a shaking of the head, the woman clearly suggesting that she leave her things there until she could locate someone to help her. Greatly relieved and thankful for this suggestion, Eva nodded at the woman, whose pleasure at having been able to help in some small way seemed genuine.

"Thank you. *Muito obrigada,*" she murmured gratefully as she turned, left behind the relative cool of the house, and emerged onto the cobblestoned street.

With sun hitting stones, the heat of the Brazilian summer's day had intensified. Eva guessed that it was at least ninety degrees, between the furnace above and the one underfoot. As quickly as she could, she proceeded to the door indicated, walking wherever possible in the shade of the houses lining both sides of the street.

She was carrying only her purse and her camera now, so she was able to take pictures as she walked. Tired as she was, she was determined to squeeze every last frame out of this trip, if only to make up for all of the trips Stu had made without her during their marriage. The street held a myriad of subjects; she captured the donkey whose lead had been draped through the door handle of a car, the two men quietly conversing at the door-jamb of one house, and some close-ups of the worn paint on a nearby windowsill. As always when she became engrossed in her picture taking, she could blot out most else taking place around her. She momentarily forgot her fatigue and her ultimate purpose on this street. Now it was only the trickle of sweat down her eyelid and the simultaneous fogging of her viewer that brought back both reality and the door before her.

Several knocks later the door was rapidly opened by a young girl, as beautiful in her native splendor as the earlier woman had been in her goodheartedness. Eva beheld a tall, slender girl, perhaps a year or two younger than herself, with dark eyes and straight black hair falling nearly to her waist, and a most remarkable glow to her bronzed skin, bordering on a blush but more deeply rooted. At the sight of Eva the girl's expression fell, confirming Eva's suspicion that the healthy glow was one of anticipation. Of whom? *Whoever it was,* mused Eva, *he had good taste.*

Intent on relieving the situation and allowing the girl to recover from her obvious disappointment, Eva began. "Do you speak English?"

The girl shrugged her shoulders, indicating that she did not and continuing to look rather downcast.

"I'm looking for a hotel. Ho-tel. Is there a hotel nearby?"

Again, an answering shrug.

"Roberto de Carvalho? Do you know where I can find Roberto de Carvalho?"

At the mention of his name, the girl's head snapped up in recognition—and something else, wondered Eva? Could this fresh young face have been looking out for the same Roberto de Carvalho? Certainly she was much too young for the middle-aged fortune hunter Eva had assumed Carvalho to be.

Conflicting emotions flickered in the girl's dark eyes, as though she was now wondering about Eva as the latter had about her. The final expression that emerged from this tug-of-war was one of benign understanding, as she gracefully signaled with her hand for Eva to go to the end of the street and then turn left.

Acknowledging the directions and hesitating to push the language barrier any further, Eva smiled, waved briefly in thank you, and moved on. *How ridiculous this is,* she thought. A goose chase within a goose chase! No street signs. No house numbers. No identification of any sort. Of course these people would all know each other, rendering such trappings of civilization unnecessary. But how was she to find her way, Eva asked herself, for the first time becoming a little uneasy and beginning to doubt the wisdom of this entire impulsive mission. She was hungry, overheated, and exhausted, perhaps as much by the tedium of the last few weeks as by the length of this trip. Craving a cool bath and a soft bed above all, she plodded on.

Turning left at the corner, Eva spotted an elderly couple about halfway down the street. Increasing her pace to intercept them before they had a chance to disappear into yet another of those azure-rimmed doorways, she waved with both hands to attract their attention as she dashed across the street. It was immediately clear to her that though the years had taken their toll physically on these two, leaving bodies bent and skin creased, there were still strong currents of life and love passing back and forth between them. As they walked, the man's arm was comfortably secured about his wife's waist in a simple gesture of support, her hand covering his there in confirmation of mutual need and appreciation.

Hesitant at disturbing this atmosphere of intimacy, Eva slowed as she reached them. The warmth and openness on their faces as they turned to her, though, gave her the courage she needed. Panting from her brief sprint in the oppressive heat, with one hand on her chest in a vain effort to slow its wild thudding, Eva once again burst into her plea.

"I'm a stranger here. I don't know my way around." *How stupid,* she chided herself. *They can see that without being able to understand me at all.*

"I need a hotel. Ho-tel." Again, she spoke the word slowly, as though they would be better able to understand the separate syllables than the whole. It was no more successful this time than it had been the last. So, she decided, she would try the name. It would be interesting to see if it evoked any reaction here.

"Roberto de Carvalho? I need to find Roberto de Carvalho. Do you know him?"

She need only have said it once, for she detected the same instant recognition of this name as she had at each previous mention of it. The man looked at his wife, who looked back at him, both expressions conveying a sense of gentle amusement as they turned their eyes back to Eva. Nodding as if in total understanding, the woman raised her arm and pointed back in the direction from which Eva had originally come. Slightly annoyed at the suggestive glances which had connected her in some intimate way with this Roberto de Carvalho, Eva was about to object when she suddenly felt too hot and weary to say another word. Smiling weakly, she retraced her steps to the house in which she had left her luggage. Instinctively, she believed that this woman would yet be able to help her.

And as misguided as her instincts had been on a few notable occasions, they were right on target now. She re-entered the house, with a brief knock on the wood of the open door, to find herself face to face with this sweet-countenanced woman, who seemed, to Eva's puzzlement, not at all surprised to see her. She did seem greatly alarmed, however, at the deterioration in Eva's physical appearance that these few minutes of streetwalking had brought about. Eva's hair was damp on her forehead and neck, her sun dress similarly clung to her, and the flush of heat and exertion that had appled her cheeks was yielding to a mild pallor.

Immediate concern clouded the woman's soft features as she jumped forward to take Eva's hand and lead her across the room, through the door, and up a narrow flight of stairs. Eva willingly let herself be drawn, sensing and appreciating this woman's maternal concern for her, believing herself to be in good hands, and too fatigued at the moment to wonder any further.

As they climbed the stairs, the woman repeatedly looked back at Eva's face as though she expected the girl to pass out at any moment. The handgrip remained firm as they reached the top of the stairs. Eva saw several doors on either side of a small hallway, one of which the woman opened and guided Eva through. Only when she was safely inside the room was Eva's hand released.

As simple and functional as the downstairs room had been, this was even more so. Immaculate and well kept, the furniture consisted of a high chest of drawers, somewhat stark but decidedly masculine, a lower table with a basin and pitcherful of water atop it and a mirror mounted on the wall behind it, and a straight-backed chair, similar to those Eva had seen below, to one side. The room was dominated, however, by the huge bed set against its longest wall and covered by a woven earth-toned spread which was now being deftly drawn back by Eva's self-appointed guardian angel. With several enthusiastic hand motions indicating that Eva was to make herself comfortable, she was suddenly gone, closing the door quietly behind her.

Reluctant to look a gift horse in the mouth after such a long day, Eva moved slowly toward the table, gingerly removing her pocketbook and her camera from her aching shoulder, and placing them down on the opposite side from the water pitcher. Looking around her, she acknowledged that she could find no hotel room more inviting than this room, though it most definitely belonged to someone else.

Bidden by curiosity, and the lack of any other personal items in the room, to examine the contents of the dresser, Eva approached it, then hesitated, before the appeal to her better nature triumphed. Intruding into someone's home, taking advantage of bed and bath was bad enough, Eva reasoned, without unnecessarily snooping.

She had never been one to hide things, had never been one to resort to stealth, although she still smarted from the afternoon, soon after her husband's death, when her father-in-law had found her cleaning out Stu's desk and had accused her of snooping in his personal affairs.

"What do you think you're doing here?" he had shot at her, after letting himself in with the key Stu had given him and thus not alerting her to his presence in the town house.

"I live here!" she had responded in a controlled tone of voice, reluctant as always to assume the worst, as it had been suggested in his own tone.

"What do you think you're doing rummaging through my son's desk?" he had rephrased the question, though not the implication.

"I have to keep myself busy and this seems like as good a place as any to do it. These papers are a mess. Perhaps if I can organize—" Eva had honestly explained her actions when Mr. Jordenson rudely interrupted her, his voice grating.

"I've heard better stories, my dear. Let's not play games with each other, shall we? You and I both know that you married Stuart for one reason. There was no love between you. That was obvious. No, you wanted his money, didn't you? I know your type. What, no rebuttal this time, innocent Eva?" he had drawled, as she stood before him with increasing disbelief, both in what he was saying and in the fact of his saying it to her now.

Eva had been too shocked at this outright accusation to respond. Instead, tears welling behind her green eyes, she had merely shaken her head, turned, and left the room. Much later, after hearing her father-in-law leave, she had crept back to neaten up those things left askew by her premature exit. The desk had been swept clean of papers, as had several of the drawers. Only one section, which had held Stu's personal correspondence, had not been touched. It was here that Eva had found the airline ticket to Rio and Roberto de Carvalho's letter.

The mention of his name in her thoughts served to pop the bubble of depression which had briefly enveloped her, and she turned to the basin on the table, filling it with the water her nameless guardian had so kindly provided. But had it in fact been provided for her? Had the woman really expected her to return? If so, how could she have known? If not, for whom had this room been prepared? Despite the absence of personal details, the room boasted a distinct sense of occupation. Who had so recently used it? Who had been about to use it again? These questions volleyed in her mind as she turned toward the inviting basin, now brimming with water.

Drawing the sun dress over her head and draping it on the chair, Eva stepped out of her high-heeled sandals and let her bare feet revel in the touch of the hard wooden floor, its even planks a welcome relief. Wearing now only bra and panties, she proceeded to sponge herself with the washcloth that she found neatly folded, along with a towel, beneath the basin. The comfort was immediate; Eva felt her muscles begin to relax as she slowly, caressingly bathed the dust and perspiration from her face, neck, and shoulders before moving on to her arms and legs. Her sponging completed, she let the washcloth slide down into the dirty water.

The relaxation had brought to Eva a heightened awareness of numbing exhaustion, so without further fuss and in the same state of undress, she dropped onto the bed, savoring the feel of the cool sheets against her still warm skin. Sleep was already making its claim as her soft auburn curls came to rest on the broad feather pillow.

Despite its promising beginning, her slumber was far from peaceful. As often happens when one has been too tense and overtired for a period, she dozed fitfully, shifting position abruptly as the various trains of thought intersected each other in her subconscious. In one moment she was back in New York playing the not-so-perfect wife to Stu's not-so-perfect husband. In another she was the grieving widow at Stu's crowded graveside, her downcast eyes mercifully hiding her innermost thoughts. In the next she was the impulsive young woman who, in silent defiance of propriety, had cast off her widow's weeds and replaced them with the brighter, more carefree wear of a vacationer. In yet another she was the attractive photographer gazing through her camera lens at the dark and compelling face of a stranger whose return scrutiny of her had touched her in some inexplicable way.

The thread was broken; she tossed again. With this last turn, however, her movement had become restricted by some mysterious weight. As consciousness phased in and out, she became aware of a figure, large and ominous, seated on the bed at her side. Sirens of alarm sounded within her as she awoke with a start, her sudden upward movement checked by cuffs of granite which encircled her upper arms, pinning her back to the bed. She had slept for several hours; the room was now lit only by the flaming streaks of the setting sun. Intermittent shadows fell long and menacing across the room. It was into one of these shadows that Eva now stared, her eyes wide with terror. From beneath the wide brim of a western-style hat, dark eyes gazed at her as they had done earlier in the day. For even in the dark shadow of his hat, Eva immediately recognized the firm jaw line, the straight nose, the high cheekbones. If she had had any doubt, the penetrating coal-black orbs which studied her now would have easily dispelled them. Indeed, the cause of Eva's present terror was none other than the man with whom she had exchanged such profound glances at the airport, the same man who had so recently been a major player in Eva's dream life.

Fear supplanting recognition once again, she began to struggle wildly to free herself from his concrete grip. Her fists pommeled his forearms with as much strength as she could muster from the elbow, her upper arms totally useless. Her bent knees managed several sound poundings of his back as she twisted madly, her body racked by spasms of panic.

"Let me go! Let me—" she began in a high-pitched scream which was abruptly cut off by a large hand firmly clamped over her mouth.

"Quiet down. You won't be hurt." His voice came at her out of the maelstrom, its firm but gentle tone making a mockery of her total panic. She sobbed and gasped for air, frantically grabbing at his wrist with the arm he had freed to silence her. When this tactic failed, she began to pound at his arm and side with such venom that he released her mouth and returned to his previous restricting grasp of her arm. Thus contained, and with a strange quivering of her limbs, her strength was suddenly spent and she could fight no longer. Looking up at her captor with eyes round in unabated terror, she lay panting, her chest heaving as she vainly attempted to control the spasmodic trembling that had overtaken her.

"It's all right. Take it easy." He repeated his earlier thoughts, but this time his tone held a velvet quality which surprisingly soothed Eva enough for her to gather her wits about her.

"Let me go. Please . . . let me go," she begged in a whisper, hoping that her tone of helplessness would appeal to his better nature, for she was sure he had one, as she recalled his gently protective attitude toward the stewardess at the airport earlier that day.

"I'll let you go when I know where you are going. Right now I rather enjoy what I see," he drawled slowly, a satanic smile spreading across thin lips as his gaze dropped from her eyes to her shoulders to her breasts, still rising and falling under her labored breathing.

At that moment, for the first time, Eva realized that she was wearing only the lace-edged bra and panties she had stripped to for her sponge bath and which she had fallen asleep in soon after. As a rosy flush erupted onto her pale cheeks, she instinctively resumed her struggle, more so in an attempt to cover herself with her arms and hands than to escape from him completely.

His hands moved to her shoulders, lifting and shaking her violently back and forth before dropping her back onto the bed and resuming his grip on her. The shaking had quieted her instantly, her only sound a swallowed sob as she again tried to control her quaking body.

"Wh-what do you want?" she stuttered through trembling lips.

"What do *you* want?" he returned, obviously enjoying the word play, its ambiguity abundantly clear to the both of them.

Eva's fear slowly began to mix with anger as she remembered her assessment of his character earlier in the day. How right she had been, she thought; an egotistical sadist, he was thoroughly enjoying this position of strength, drawing out both her fear and her embarrassment.

Mustering what little strength remained, she determined to play at his game. In a tone as bold and confident as she could produce, she demanded, "Get out of my room. How dare you barge in here like this. You have no right. I insist you leave now or I'll scream again . . . and I doubt the lady of this house would permit you here in the first place."

This she had added in a last-ditch effort to re-establish some touch with a reality she felt she was losing. For this man had begun to have a strange and unexpected effect on her. No longer fearing for her life, her main concern had become fear of something even more dangerous and infinitely more two-sided. She had become shockingly aware of this man's physical presence so near her. His face was no more that a few inches away, his torso at a shallow angle to her prone form, their bodies touching at the hips as he sat, and the hands as he continued to restrain her. She was acutely conscious of his musky male smell, the firm contours of his body above her, the steady penetration of his eyes to her, through her, into her very essence.

As though reading the subtle change in her green eyes, now glittering in a jumble of confusion, apprehension, and excitement, his face moved slowly toward hers, a deliberately provocative movement. Eva inhaled to protest in vain as his lips seized hers, forcing them into silence, dominating them, crushing them with the force of brute animal instinct. His lips released hers as deliberately as they had taken them, a stark statement that only his willing it had terminated the contact.

Eva lay in shocked silence as though in a world totally apart from the one in which she had so recently been widowed. Her mind told her to resist; her body refused. Never before had she been kissed with such conviction. Her lips burned in the aftermath of his fiery possession; her insides quivered in the memory of it.

She shook her head from side to side, as if to deny the chemical reaction which had already begun, but when he moved again to still her resistance, she yielded willingly to the seering need that had been building within her for months and months, and now threatened to rage out of control.

As his lips covered hers once again, she responded to him with an urgency she could no longer contain. Sensing this need, his kiss softened into one no longer of forceful domination but of subtle challenge, as the gentle pressure of his lips parted hers in a soul-reaching massage. His hands had released their grip on her arms and were now caressing her every contour, fingers tracing the line of her jaw, her ear lobe, cascading down the sensitive cord of her neck to her shoulder. One hand returned to stroke her cheek as the other glided to her waist, its thumb faintly brushing the swell of her breast in its volatile descent.

An involuntary moan of pleasure escaped her lips as her hands, of their own volition, climbed to his shoulders in eager exploration of his taut-muscled frame, before intertwining with the thick crop of black hair at the nape of his neck. In this moment of passion she blocked out all else but the mutual hunger being assuaged by and for this man whose name she didn't know.

As reciprocal as their lovemaking had been, so was this shock of reality as he roughly thrust her away from him and abruptly stood and walked across the room to the window. Eva bolted into a seated position, her feet dangling on the floor, her head collapsed on her chest, her wildly beating heart the only sound audible to her as she tried to assimilate into her consciousness the events of the last few minutes. In a gesture of self-defense, though from whom she was not sure, she reached for and quickly put on the sun dress she had so casually removed earlier.

The sun had fallen surreptitiously behind the mountains during this physical interchange, leaving the barest remnant of the golden edging which had but moments before outlined the craggy peaks. Eva glanced sidelong at the stranger, now dispassionately staring at this thread of nature. How controlled he was, she thought, becoming painfully aware of her own shortcomings in that department.

In a voice soft and unsure, she broke the silence in search of the answer to the only question that had surfaced amid the passionate whirlpool of earlier moments.

"Who are you?"

The tall stranger, if she could now truthfully call him that, turned pensively toward her, his gaze coming to rest on her questioning eyes.

"Who are *you*?" Once again the game, she thought. Damn him. But someone had to give first and she was not one to carry pride to absurdity.

"My name is Eva Jordenson. I'm here on an expedition into the Serra do Espinhaco." Reluctant to reveal too much, though she found the words slipping out too easily for comfort, she sighed as she asked a final time, slowly and deliberately, "Who are you?"

The answer came back crisp, bold, and determined, with the pride that a particular set of the chin had suggested once before.

"I am Roberto de Carvalho."

CHAPTER 3

Stunned silence filled the room as Eva stared in disbelief. "Who?" she burst out, the shock in her voice shattering the fragile atmosphere.

This time the response held a note of impatience, almost anger. "I am Roberto de Carvalho." For the first time, in the pronunciation of his name, Eva detected the trace of an accent. His English had been otherwise flawless, the spilling of words from his tongue so spontaneous that it had not occurred to her that this was anyone but a fellow countryman. His dress, too, was strictly contemporary and very American. In complement to the wide-brimmed hat of a far finer material than those of the local peasants she had seen on the road, he wore a khaki-colored cotton shirt, rolled to the elbow and open at the throat, dark blue jeans which skimmed his lean hips and muscular thighs in rugged harmony of man and material, and sturdy leather boots whose richness seeped through even the fresh layer of dust. A very American look, yet the articulation of his name defied this image, perplexing Eva all the more. He had spoken his name with a sense of pride, both personal and national; she respected him for it, even as she found it electrifying.

Eva had been staring at him, tongue-tied, a rare experience for her. As she sought her next words, he barked through thin drawn lips.

"I know of no Eva Jordenson on this trip! Who are you?"

"Eva Jordenson—er, Mrs. Stuart Jordenson. You met my husband in New York and made arrangements with him for this expedition?"

"Yes, of course, I met a Stuart Jordenson and he did plan to join this group. But he made no mention of a wife, much less of plans to bring her here." The anger in his voice took her aback, and she suddenly wished she had written beforehand informing him of her intentions. In her own desperate need to escape New York, it had not occurred to her that joining the expedition would pose any problem. Dismayed at her own shortsightedness and not quite sure where to begin her explanation, she once again found herself directed by a low-toned question.

"Where is your husband?"

Strangely embarrassed, Eva looked away from him quickly. "Stu is dead. He suffered a heart attack two weeks ago. I had assumed that I could take his place." The words had come too fast, and she riveted her eyes toward him in anxious anticipation of his reaction. She was totally unprepared for it when it came.

Two broad strides brought him from his position before the window to where she stood by the dresser. Barely masking the contempt etched in fine lines around his mouth, he cruelly seized her by the shoulders, spinning her around until her back was to the bed. Anger seethed as he growled, low and threatening.

"Just what kind of imbecile do you take me for? A more callous story I've never heard before! You'd like to have me believe that a mere two weeks after your husband's sudden and premature—if my judgment of his age and health last month were correct—death, you hop a plane and show up thousands of miles away in a small town at the edge of nowhere, intending to join an expedition to which you were neither invited nor are wanted? I don't believe you, Mrs. . . . whatever your name might be. Don't tell me about the recent death of your husband when this is mine for the taking—"

He thrust his hand roughly into the mass of curls, pulling her head back precariously as he drew her slim body against his and fiercely claimed her lips once more. This time there was neither tenderness nor persuasion; it was a raw act of possession, reducing the potential of beauty to its basest form. The message was clear to Eva as she was forced to endure his punishing kiss. When he finally released her, she staggered backward, sitting down hard on the edge of the bed. Fear permeated her every fiber, not so much of Roberto de Carvalho as of what he had said. In her heart she felt that his accusations were justified. What kind of a wanton could she be to have behaved such? An inner torment had begun to gnaw at her, and Eva felt her confidence disintegrating.

Roberto now stood in the middle of the room, his hands on his hips, his broad stance one of the master awaiting an accounting for some heinous crime. He was not going to make it any easier for her this time, as his steady gaze bore into her in silent expectation.

Eva's eyes had been glued to his in confusion and fear since his violent demonstration. She shifted them now toward her pocketbook, which rested on the low table where she had placed it earlier. As in a trance she went to it, reached inside, and drew out the strongest pieces of evidence she had—her passport and the letter from Roberto which had traveled so many miles and back again. Shoulders bent in a posture of defeat, she handed him the two items before moving to the opposite side of the bed where she sank down, her back to him, a fresh outburst of trembling racking her body. Wrapping her arms around herself protectively, she began to rock gently back and forth, suddenly overwhelmed by the torment of the past few weeks, indeed the past hour. For the first time since she awoke to Roberto's presence, she was completely unaware of him, her only sense being the intensity of the pain which radiated from within to her every extremity. She was conscious of a low, tortured sob, though unaware that it had escaped her own lips.

At the moment her anguish peaked to shatter the last shreds of control, strong yet gentle arms enveloped her, drawing her into a cocoon of warmth and tenderness. With her head buried between a firm hand and powerful chest, the tears that had been denied for so long would be denied no longer. Roberto held her as she yielded to the convulsive sobs that shook her. Tears streaked down her cheeks, soaking his shirt, a protective hand pressing her closer to him as he stroked her head soothingly. His body adopted the steady sway, to and fro, which hers had begun, and he patiently let her cry until the vehemence of her grief was spent.

Eva did not know how long she remained thus, cradled in Roberto's arms, absorbing the comfort he offered. When the worst of the quivering had subsided and the tears had ceased, she withdrew from his arms and moved to the window, where she stood gazing out at the darkened hills. In a voice broken intermittently by the uneven rhythm of a few lingering sobs, she spoke.

"I had to get away. You c-can't imagine the oppression there. I couldn't die beside Stuart, although they would have liked it. I f-found your letter among Stu's papers and it seemed like a perfect solution at the t-time. Maybe I was wrong. Was I?"

She reeled around with a force she hadn't realized she still possessed and glared at him, her voice gaining in strength. "Was I wrong? I'm human, too. I was never unfaithful to my husband. I am *not* some merry widow looking for a good time. I *need* some time—to think, to relax, to work." Glancing around, she pointed a shaky finger at her camera, as she rapidly continued.

"I'm a photographer. I work. I am competent. I do my job well. My photography gives me great comfort. I saw this expedition as a photographic opportunity that would be good for me. So I took it." She spoke quickly, as though fearing that these thoughts which so begged to be aired would be lost somehow if she hesitated.

"I'm sorry if I sound foolish. Believe me, I can give as much as the next. And I'm happy to do so. But right now *I* need this trip." Trying to anticipate his arguments, she continued her monologue.

"I can handle it physically, if that's what worries you." Here she felt the color rise to her cheek as her mind retraced her most recent physical endeavor. Too quickly, she went on.

"I can climb those hills, search old caves, cook—whatever you ask of the others I can match. Please give me the chance."

The poignancy of her final plea was not unappreciated. Through the long moments of her rebuttal, he had sat transfixed. Unfathomable at their murky depths, his eyes never left hers. Now, with the silence looming as a heavy mist between them, he rose from the bed and walked toward the door, his gaze only then shifting.

"Be downstairs in twenty minutes. You can meet the

others then. While we eat I will outline our route." The strangely husky voice broke off, and he was gone before Eva could begin to respond.

She stood in the wake of his departure staring at the door whose closing click had brought with it a ring of finality to the issue. Slowly, she let out the breath she had been holding. She raised her hand to her chest to steady her racing heartbeat, realizing how close she had come to losing out on the main objective of this trip. If Roberto de Carvalho had denied her request to accompany the group into the hills tomorrow, she would have been defeated in this first effort to rebuild her life. True, she had gotten away from New York, had begun to sample the healing warmth of this far-away country, and had already taken many photographs which she could proudly present to her editor. But the Espinhaco Topaz would be the *pièce de résistance,* she knew. It would add an overall direction to the photographs she collected here. It would be a breathtaking subject in and of itself. Yes, the Espinhaco Topaz would be the climax of her journey . . . or so she had thought.

Strange and disquieting thoughts began to race in Eva's brain. What was she really doing here? She had run away from the problems besieging her in New York. She couldn't fool herself any longer—she had run away, something she had never done in her life. She had been raised to be a fatalist, facing challenges with a calm acceptance. What was happening to her now?

More perplexing, what had happened to her a few minutes ago in the arms of a total stranger? By all rights she should have been indignant at Roberto's approach, rejecting his advances, even fighting them off as the cheap and degrading portents of a lust to which she suspected that type of man was accustomed. He hadn't been satisfied with the passing stewardess; Eva had catapulted into his expedition and he would take advantage of the effect which, he was sure to know by now, he had on her. She must be constantly on her guard, she resolved.

But whom did she fear? Roberto? Or herself. Eva sat down on the bed at this last admission, studying the folded-back coverlet and the indentations that had so recently been made by two bodies, side by side in intimate embrace. She let her eyes roam back toward the pillow, from which her head had risen to meet his in a moment of uncontrolled passion. What had come over her? She had never been one to behave in such a reckless manner.

Always before, she had been able to monitor her emotions. She couldn't deny that Stu had excited her. He had introduced her to the art of lovemaking with the tenderness and consideration born of experience. Eva had often wondered, especially as their mutual attraction had begun to fade, how she compared with his other conquests. As for her, although she had none to compare with, she had been pleased with the initial intimacy, sensing the thrill of an arousal which, though falling short of a deeper ecstasy she could fantasize about, complimented her feelings of femininity.

It was with chagrin that Eva recalled the burgeoning passion that this stranger named Roberto de Carvalho had ignited within her. Never before had she been stirred to the height to which his overpowering masculinity and raw sensuousness had carried her. She blushed even now at the eagerness of her response, vividly remembering the shock of separation when the embrace had been broken.

At the time, she had attributed her shock to the plain fact of his assault. Now, as her lips tingled in remembrance of the firm and persuasive touch of his, she knew it was something deeper—it was her own driving need that shocked and bewildered her as much as his. She would have to guard her own actions, as well as his, for should she give in to this newly discovered susceptibility, she feared that the psychological damage to her own fragile state of mind would be irreparable.

Complicating the situation further, Eva was totally bewildered by her behavior after the embrace. Why had she broken down, crying like a baby, in this man's presence? What had come over her? She couldn't remember the last time she had let herself go emotionally to such an extent in front of someone else. She was a very private person, and self-control had always been a characteristic she prized, though she was well aware that it may have hurt her marriage. If she had been able to talk more with Stu, maybe things would have been different. Instead, she had bottled up all the anger and bitterness until she seethed at everything he said and did. Why had she restrained herself with her husband and then collapsed before Roberto, a stranger? The question nagged at her mercilessly.

Looking at her watch, Eva saw that her twenty minutes were nearly gone. Frantically scanning the room, it hit her suddenly that she did not have her other bags, that they must still be downstairs where she had left them earlier. Refusing to be daunted by this minor setback, she straightened the bed with a sweep of the hand before grabbing the wet washcloth from the basin, wringing it out, and applying it to her eyes, which still bore signs of the tears that had so violently overflowed. Fortunately, her pocketbook held a few items of makeup; hastily repairing the damage to her eyeliner and mascara, she restored the red-purple gleam to her lips, added a stroke of rhubarb to the hollows of her cheeks, and brushed her wayward curls into a semblance of casual disorder. Replacing these items into her pocketbook, she put on a pair of gradient red-tinted eyeglasses, used primarily for reading when her eyes were strained, which would serve perfectly to hide the slight puffiness that lingered around her eyes. With a final straightening tug at her sun dress, she grimaced into her high-heeled sandals, gathered the shoulder straps of her pocketbook and camera together, and left the room.

Retracing the steps she had taken earlier, Eva easily found the living room, which she assumed to be the site of this gathering. Her hunch was correct. As she appeared at the doorway of this front room, conversation was already in progress among a group of men—several standing, several seated on and around the sills of the elongated windows that overlooked the street. There were four men in all, two of whom conversed in low tones in a language Eva guessed to be French from the few word fragments that the evening breeze gently carried to her across the room. Both men were of above-average height and athletic build, though one was fair-skinned and auburn-haired while the other was dark, a well-trimmed black beard accentuating the immediate sense of mystery, even threat, which sent a brief shiver through Eva. The other two were somewhat younger, perhaps in their early twenties, she guessed. Both had an American Ivy-League look about them, from their faded jeans and open-necked Oxford cloth shirts to their loafer-shod feet. One, a sandy-haired fellow with a friendly look, had a pullover sweater draped around his shoulders, prompting Eva to note for the future the potential of the evening breeze. The last young man was lean as his buddy had been, but he was darker, his thick brown hair falling carelessly across his forehead. Eva was struck by something very familiar in his face, a feature she couldn't pinpoint but which distinctly reminded her of someone else—though she wasn't sure of whom.

The conversations had continued during her brief, and unobserved, evaluation of the group from the doorway. Not one to flaunt her own good looks, Eva was nevertheless aware that she did present a pretty picture as she stood thus beneath the door frame. Whatever she lacked internally in the absence of a fresh change of clothes was well compensated on the surface by those she wore. The stylish sun dress, yellow with a delicate flowered pattern in pinks and roses, contrasted effectively with her brown-red hair, its curls soft and full around her face, their circular tendrils echoed in the round-framed glasses, whose color coordinated perfectly with the floral print of her dress. Now the younger dark-haired man glanced up and spotted her, a warm smile overspreading his features as he jumped out of his relaxed stance against the window frame and came forward to greet her.

"Mrs. Jordenson, welcome!" he began, the warmth of his smile echoed in his soft voice and immediately spreading to Eva, who had felt some trepidation at confronting her fellow travelers for the first time. Relieved to hear English automatically spoken, she extended her hand to meet his firm grasp, finding comfort in his sincerity. It dawned on her that he must be an insider here, to have expected her, even known her name on such short notice.

"I'm Paul Sanders. I don't believe you know any of the others." He drew her confidently into the room toward them, one hand remaining lightly at her back as he made the introductions.

"Eva Jordenson . . . Jacques Laurent." He gestured toward the auburn-haired man, his name confirming her suspicion of his origin. The latter smiled easily, his eyes lighting his features as he took her hand in his.

"I'm very pleased to meet you, Eva. And very pleased you'll be joining us," he added in beautifully accented English, a twinkle in his eye to match the image of the debonair Parisian.

Paul's hand gestured again. "Pierre Langelier," he moved on, the second Frenchman nodding in silent acknowledgment but making no movement toward her other than the ominous glare his eyes threw in her direction. Quickly, as if to escape some impending disaster, Eva turned her attention to the final face, that of the sandy-haired young man, who had now arisen from his seat to greet her.

"Tom Allen . . . Mrs. Jordenson." Was it a hint of warning which Eva detected in this last, more formal introduction? Shrugging it off as her imagination, she met the smile and the hand which were offered.

"How are you, Tom?" she added warmly.

"Ah, she has a voice!" burst back Tom, his infectious grin setting the tone. "I'm just fine, now that you're here. Do you know that my friend Paul, here, had the gall to imply that this was an all-male expedition? Imagine that! Can you see me spending four days in deserted mountains with only these faces for company?" As he looked in mock panic from one face to the other, Eva laughed aloud, the first time she had done so in ages, she realized. Yes, this trip would be good for her!

Returning his friendly banter, she explained, "It was a last-minute decision on my part to come, so Paul was not entirely mistaken. As a photographer, I couldn't turn down the opportunity." She carefully avoided the hint of any other reasons for her presence. "What is your motive?" she added, eager both to learn something of the others and to keep up the easy conversation.

Tom went on, "I'm on intersession from law school.

My roommate here conned me into this little jaunt. For my health, he says!" His smile fell on Paul good-naturedly, before his eyes returned to wink at Eva.

"Don't let him kid you. A greater adventurer I've never met! In fact, I probably wouldn't be here myself had it not been for Tom's enthusiasm," retorted Paul, humor softening his words.

Aware that the two Frenchmen were following, though not participating in, the exchange, Eva turned to the more pleasant of the two, Jacques. Phrasing her question to apply to them both, and thus avoiding a further query to Pierre, whose grimness made her uneasy, she ventured, "You are French, I gather?"

"Oui, madame," began Jacques with a sweep of the arm across his waist in a confirming bow. "Pierre and I are business acquaintances. I live in Paris; Pierre is from Tours," he explained amenably.

In a mock whisper audible to all, Tom leaned toward Eva. "You'll have to excuse Pierre. He doesn't say much to beautiful young ladies."

As though in answer to the challenge, a deep, harsh voice broke into the discussion. "And where is the beautiful young lady's husband?" he taunted, his heavy accent barely disguising the undertone.

Eva knew that she would have to learn to cope with this inevitable question. "My husband is dead," she stated simply, defiance in her eyes as she met Pierre's. They definitely rubbed each other the wrong way, Eva knew—a sad way to start an expedition such as this.

A heavy silence besieged the conversation. At that moment all eyes riveted to the front door as Roberto de Carvalho strode boldly into the house. His mere physical presence dominated all others—a born leader, begrudged Eva, even as he broke the aura of tension which had formed.

The wide-brimmed hat was gone, laying open his

features for Eva's inspection. As from the first time she had set eyes on him, she was stunned by his good looks and oozing masculinity. He had not changed his clothes since their encounter upstairs; here, the bright lights emphasized the broad lines of his chest, the leanness of his torso, the power of his denim-clad legs.

Roberto's eye caught and held hers for a brief moment, their dark expression an enigma to Eva. Fearing the rebirth of the stirrings within her, she tore her gaze from him, diverting it to Paul in subtle suggestion. But it was Roberto who spoke first, taking the lead as she knew he would, in his smoothly commanding tone.

"I assume that everyone has met. I've just made a final check on our supplies; everything seems to be in order. We'll have dinner now. While we eat I can fill you in on the details of our expedition and answer any questions you may have." Having thus said his piece, he added, "Please follow me," and headed through the doorway.

The group filed one by one down the long, narrow hall toward the furthermost area of the house, the customary placement of the kitchen in the tropics to isolate the heat of cooking as much as possible from the other rooms. Roberto had gone first; Eva managed, in spite of gentlemanly gestures by the others, to maneuver the two Frenchmen ahead of her, putting a much-needed buffer between Roberto and herself.

The kitchen was a spacious room, dominated by open windows, wide countertops, and a large rectangular table set in the middle. Eva was immediately enchanted by it, admiring the feeling of ease, openness, and relaxation which it urged. And adding to her pleasure was the sight of the lovely little woman, her own guardian angel, she mused, who had been so kind to her earlier. From her position before the cast-iron stove, this plump figure threw Eva a friendly smile and secretive wink before turning her attention back to the food she was busily spooning into serving dishes. Without a moment's hesitation, Eva moved forward to lend a hand with the transfer of the food to the table, when she was abruptly caught by the elbow and firmly escorted to a place at the table. Silent but questioning eyes traced the arm from her elbow up past a sinewy shoulder into the face of Roberto, whose oddly fierce expression bade her sit before he forced her down himself. Annoyed by his interference—but in truth more puzzled by his apparent impatience with her—she sat, thereby permitting the others, with what she thought was inappropriate formality, to do the same.

The tempting aroma wafting from the freshly prepared food startled Eva with the realization of how hungry she was. The last food she had eaten had been the early lunch airborne between Rio and Belo. How much had happened between then and now! But Eva was determined not to let her thoughts get bogged down again, so she turned her concentration to the food and the company.

Throughout the meal Roberto graciously played the host, explaining the nature and origin of each local dish, which was served quite ably by Maria, as she was introduced. Eva was doubly appreciative of this information; not only did it satisfy her innate curiosity but it enabled her to subtly avoid eating any fish. A generally healthy person, she invariably suffered a violent allergic reaction when she consumed fish of any kind, regardless of its preparation. The main dish served this evening, a Brazilian specialty called *feijoada,* had contained many ingredients she could not recognize through the thick black gravy. Despite its mouth-watering smell, Eva hesitated to sample it until Roberto detailed its ingredients: black beans, beef, pork, tomatoes, and spices, at which point she dug in with relish, savoring every bite. Although she carried a strong prescriptive drug with her at all times to counteract the allergy should she mistakenly ingest any fish, she didn't want Roberto de Carvalho to know of this weakness. She knew that it would only bolster his first impression of her, which she was determined to prove wrong.

To Eva's surprise and pleasure the evening passed quite enjoyably, with an absence of the awkwardness that might have existed within a group such as this, coming together for the first time on the eve of a trip destined to throw them into intimate association with each other. Small talk dominated most of the early conversation, the casual talk giving each a taste of the background of the others. Eva chatted comfortably with various members of the group, finding herself most at ease with Paul. They discussed subjects that involved a minimum of controversy, such as photography; traveling; New York, which Eva knew so well; Boston, where Paul and Tom attended law school; and the relative merits of hiking boots, which Paul had brought, and sneakers, which Eva had brought.

Eva carefully avoided Roberto's eyes, particularly at moments when she felt his gaze burning through her. Fortunately, although he sat at the head of the table and was clearly the host, the Ivy-Leaguers, Paul and Tom, managed between the two of them to keep the level of conversation fast and the humor high. Jacques joined the discussions frequently, his voice deep and melodious with its gentle accent. Pierre, on the other hand, remained aloof, adding a word here or a grunt there, but never opening up as the others had done.

At the conclusion of the meal and with the obligatory serving of *cafèzinho,* Roberto turned the discussion deftly toward what clearly excited him more than photography, traveling, New York, Boston, or footwear—namely, the details of the expedition. As the six sat around the table, cleared now of all dishes save the tiny coffee cups that Maria continually refilled, he proceeded to outline the plans.

"We'll be leaving at dawn tomorrow, which means that you should pack tonight. We've got four donkeys for use as pack animals. Each of you will have one knapsack to hold whatever personal items you will need. Remember, you carry your own pack, so beware of its weight." This last he directed pointedly at Eva, much to her mortification. "Bring only the absolute necessities—a change of clothes, a towel, a few cosmetic items. You'll need a sweater or jacket of some sort, since it can get cool at night. But the days will be hot as we climb, so choose accordingly. With a little luck we won't get caught in a downpour. Although they do occur during this season, it's not worth dragging along heavy rain gear just in case. A little rain won't hurt any of us, especially after sweating in the heat for several days." A faint snicker interrupted him. For herself, Eva was grateful for her tinted lenses which hid her slight embarrassment at his bluntness.

"I've got a sleeping bag for each of you and an ample supply of food and water for the four or five days we should be gone," he continued. "The main burden for the pack animals will be the equipment we will need when we reach the mine." Here he paused to draw a dog-eared piece of paper, yellowed with age and bearing the distinct tracings of coffee-cup stains, from the western-style pocket of his shirt.

Eva's eye had followed the hand-to-chest movement, lingering on the latter long after the other eyes had turned to the map. Roberto's monopolization of this part of the conversation had enabled her to study him freely, outwardly as the others were doing but inwardly in a quite different manner. She noted his posture, casual yet alert, a statement to the world of his continuous involvement. Her eyes roamed the breadth of his chest, resting on the dark hairs that had escaped the confines of his shirt in its narrow vee, before climbing the tanned column of his strong neck to alight on his now animated face. *He looks almost boyish,* she thought, *when he enjoys what he's doing, obviously the case right now.* Eva smiled with an affection that startled her, her mind nowhere near the map, which the others were so seriously studying. At that moment Roberto glanced up at her. Her smile vanished immediately, replaced by a slight flush of the cheek. His expression held a note of amusement and mockery, his eyes sending her a private message which only increased her blush. With as much conviction as she could muster, she turned her attention away from Roberto and onto the map that was to lead the small group of mountain wanderers to the Espinhaco Topaz.

Study of the map completed, Roberto refolded it and returned it to his pocket—the latter movement with a smirk toward Eva, as if he had been aware of her personal wanderings from the start—and excused himself to disappear into one of the rooms off the long hallway that led to the kitchen. When he re-emerged he carried a pile of large canvas and nylon knapsacks, which he unceremoniously dumped onto the center of the table for each to help himself. He then answered the few questions raised, none of which concerned Eva directly.

"If there are no other questions," he began, looking slowly from face to face around the table, "I suggest we turn in. Remember, dawn tomorrow!"

It suddenly occurred to Eva that she had a whole list of questions, some critical to her—such as where her luggage was, because she hadn't seen it earlier in the living room—which needed answering.

"Wait!" she burst out, looking in embarrassment at

the five faces turned toward her in surprise. "Ah . . . I have several questions. The hotel? I need a place to sleep. And my luggage? I seem to have misplaced it." She paused, feeling like an idiot, wishing desperately that these men would stop looking so intently at her, magnifying her feeling of incompetency.

"I think, Mrs. Jordenson," Roberto's cool tone broke into her state of discomposure, the mocking twist of his lips at the corner of his mouth only intensifying it, "that we should let the others go now. They must be tired. I can answer any questions for you after they leave."

Damn him! Damn him! Just what I don't want, and he knows it, she thought, but she gave a forced smile and a terse nod of assent.

"Thank you. I'd appreciate that."

One by one the men offered congenial "good nights" and departed, heading toward who-knows-where, thought Eva, and leaving her alone with Roberto.

CHAPTER 4

Eva and Roberto stood staring at each other in silence as the last of the footsteps faded into the distance. Eva held her tongue, waiting for him to initiate the conversation as she knew he would. Not disappointing her, his coolly impersonal but polite tone broke into the stillness.

"Would you like more coffee?" To her surprise he did not wait for a reply but proceeded to clear the empty cups from the table, Maria having left unobtrusively a short time before. Eva made no effort to help him, since he had rebuffed her earlier offering of help to Maria, and she was curious to see the extent of his custodial ability. It seemed that his offer of more coffee had indeed been a formality, for he adeptly washed all of the cups, leaving them to drain dry at the side of the sink. Eva was already feeling the stimulating effect of the espresso, so she would have refused more given the chance. Now, as she watched him finish his cleanup of the kitchen, she felt her annoyance melt away, to be replaced by faint amusement at this unexpected touch of domesticity.

"Do I entertain you?" he spoke, glimpsing Eva's expression. "It seems to be becoming a habit of mine," this last in reference to the moment earlier that evening when she had similarly smiled at his actions. Eva chose to ignore the implication.

"I enjoy seeing a man who can handle so-called woman's work. Most men I know would have broken half the dishes before they ever reached the sink, let alone gotten them clean as you have," she replied, gaining confidence as she talked to this man whose presence vaguely intimidated her.

He gave a sideways nod, lifting one eyebrow as he did. "If that was meant to be a compliment, I thank you. But then, I'm not like most men you know, am I?" The gently teasing tone that now entered the conversation excited Eva, despite silent protestations in the back of her mind. Was it the caffeine or this other source of stimulation that was responsible for the trembling of her innards, she wondered.

"No, you're not," she conceded. But how could he have known that? Could he have sensed the awakening flames within her at his very glance? Or had something of the surprise and even fear she had felt at her own outpouring of passion in his arms given her away? "But then, I really know nothing about you," she went on, attempting to cover herself. As much as she wanted to protect herself from him, Eva felt herself drawn inexorably toward him like a moth to a flame.

Roberto's stance, as he leaned back against the sink, shaggy-haired forearms piggybacked on his chest, was relaxed, compatible with the conversation. He seemed to have mellowed in her presence also, to the point even of enjoying her company. The strange surge of affection she felt as she faced him thus frightened her. Determined to blanket herself in some less personal direction, she ventured, "How did you meet the others? Are they business contacts, as was my husband?" The change of subject, and particularly the mention of Stu, had its desired effect. Roberto's expression became more serious and impersonal.

"Jacques and I met last year at a conference in Paris. He was one of the keynote speakers; we spent quite a bit of time talking. Pierre is Jacques's friend. I've never met him before."

"Pierre makes me very uncomfortable. He seems so angry and bitter. I wonder why?" she thought aloud, half regretting her forwardness, half hoping that Roberto might have some explanation to alleviate her nagging uneasiness in Pierre's presence.

"Jacques mentioned something about an unhappy marriage. Relax . . . I doubt you have anything to fear from Pierre." Again the smirk.

"I'm sure," she retorted, annoyed at the transparency of her feelings. Moving to safer ground, she went on. "What about Tom and Paul. How do you know them? Certainly they're not business associates!"

"They go to school in Boston. I happen to spend a good deal of time there." A slight evasiveness had crept into this response. "Do you like them?" His interest seemed to be genuine.

"They're terrific. Tom is quite a character. What a great sense of humor. Paul could probably become a best friend . . . if I lived in Boston," she responded enthusiastically. This last brought an even deeper grin to Roberto's face, altering his jaw line enough to jolt Eva by its familiarity. Impulsively she burst out, "Do you know that there is a resemblance between you and Paul? When I first saw him I knew there was something familiar in his expression. Now I see it . . . the jaw line especially, but also the nose and the cheekbones. His coloring is a little lighter, but you could be brothers!" The words had flowed freely, spontaneously, as Eva had herself seen the similarity.

"We are." Short and simple as was his style, Roberto made his statement smugly and then awaited Eva's reaction.

Beneath its curls Eva's forehead creased where her eyebrows drew together in a look of incomprehension. Roberto's head flew back in a burst of unconstrained laughter.

"But the names . . . he's so young . . . he made no mention . . ." she stammered, trying to justify her puzzlement.

"Paul is my half-brother. We have the same mother. Because of the age difference and the fact of different fathers continents apart, we don't have the intimacy that years together in a family might create. But we've become much closer recently. I like Paul. I'm glad that you do." The genuine feeling for Paul apparent in Roberto's words and facial expression touched Eva. For whatever he was or was not worth as a ladies' man, she suspected that he had a genuine streak of warmth for his family, past and future.

The glint of humor had returned to Roberto's eyes. "So you think I'm an old man, do you?"

"By all means," Eva gave a backward denial, even as she admired anew the touch of gray at his sideburns. Her fingertips ached to reach over and explore the silvery ends, but she restrained herself. Fearing that the conversation was again taking on too personal an overtone, she changed the subject.

"My questions. For starters, where is a hotel? I walked all over this afternoon with no luck in finding it."

"You're here," he grinned, appreciating her sudden attempt to lead the conversation to safer lines.

"This is no hotel," she argued, beginning to resent the amusement he found at her expense, "and I need some place to stay tonight. I'm really tired."

With unexpected impatience Roberto restated the fact. "This is as close as you'll come to a hotel in Terra Vermelho. It is my home. The other men are quartered in other homes. Actually, Paul was to have stayed here with me, but I rearranged things when you so conveniently, or inconveniently as the case may prove to be, fell into my lap." A smile flittered across his lips briefly. "You'll stay in my room, as you did this afternoon. Yes, I went to my own room after a long trip, only to find my bed already occupied."

As understanding slowly dawned, Eva felt sharp anger that he had not explained all this sooner. He went on before she could voice her objections.

"My housekeeper, Maria, rightly assumed that you were my guest when you repeatedly mentioned my name. She was not expecting a woman, though, and unfortunately jumped to the wrong conclusion."

"I'll say!" Eva interjected defensively. "So she showed me to your bed and then very diligently ushered you up as soon as you came in. Very accommodating." Sarcasm threw a look of disdain onto her features. "I'm sure she's used to that sort of thing!"

"If I didn't know that you were so recently—and tragically—widowed, I'd say you were jealous," he returned her sarcasm with his own, a wicked gleam in his eye.

Not knowing, much to her own consternation, an appropriate response, Eva chose once again to ignore his suggestion. "My luggage . . . I had two bags. Where are they?"

"In my . . . ah, your room. They were put away after you arrived. Paul just brought them upstairs."

Eva felt momentary panic as her mind jumped

further on. Uncannily, Roberto remained a step ahead of her.

"No, I won't be sharing your bed this night, as much as I might wish it. You know, you do look beautiful." His stance shifted suddenly as he straightened and approached her. "I think you must be fully recovered by now," he smirked, reaching up to remove the eyeglasses which had served their purpose.

So he had seen through her again, Eva knew. What power did he have over her, she wondered with increasing alarm, this roguish adventurer?

His hand returned to finger the gentle curls that cascaded around her ear lobe. He now stood within inches of her, his eyes gazing down at her in gentle caress. Slowly and seductively his gaze slid from her rounded eyes across her cheekbone and around the sweep of her jaw to her moist lips. His eyes had made passionate love to her, and she gasped almost imperceptively at the excitement they evoked.

Then, the hand that had teased her hair dropped abruptly to his side as he stepped back from her, the only evidence of any emotion the slight irregularity of his breathing. The trance was broken. Eva's head jerked back as though suddenly released from a binding grip, though there had been none. Devastated by his rejection and frustrated by unfulfilled desires, Eva steeled herself against any words that might come.

Taking a deep breath, a look of anger now in his eyes, he growled under his breath, low and husky, "The widow is a siren! A damned siren! I'm stuck with a bewitching siren!"

Eva's own anger and hurt could be controlled no longer. In an instant she swung her hand up to deliver a solid slap to his face. Its impact took him by surprise, but his reflexes were sharp enough to capture her wrist in its descent, and, jerking it behind her back, he joined it with the other, thus pinioning her stiffened body against the lean, hard contours of his. Distraught as she was, Eva couldn't miss the musky smell of him as he pressed her closer to him. Her head was tilted back to look at him as he growled slowly through gritted teeth.

"You are a nuisance and a temptation which I don't need. I won't have my expedition sabotaged by some sex-starved black widow. You can cast your web elsewhere. But, so help me, if you hurt anyone here, you'll regret having ever come to Brazil. Do you understand?" He tightened his arms sharply, as though to force her compliance. "Do you understand? And don't pull that pathetic teary-eyed routine on me again. I don't make the same mistake twice."

The last he added at the appearance of tears brimming on Eva's eyelids. As he thrust her away from him, she fought to restrain both the tears and the knot of nausea in the pit of her stomach, brought on by his sudden violence.

But the instinct for survival was strong in Eva. She would not let herself be put down by this brute. Eyes sparkling now with anger and determination, she lashed back at him.

"I have every right to be here! My place was duly reserved and my supplies paid for. I see no difference whether a woman fills it or a man, although you seem to be hung up on that issue. Furthermore, I have no designs on anyone here. I haven't the emotional strength for that right now. But you wouldn't know what I'm talking about. And what makes you think that you or someone else here has anything I want? I find you despicable!"

Not quite sure how far to push her luck, Eva paused in time to notice a subtle softening of Roberto's expression, and the return of a light to eyes that moments before had been fathomless black pits. His faint smile held a touch of sadness, which tore at Eva's heart in spite of what she had just said. In that instant she would have run to comfort him in her arms, as he had done earlier for her. The venom had evaporated as quickly as it had gathered, though for the life of her, Eva didn't know how.

Roberto's voice retained a note of that sadness. "As long as we understand each other, Mrs. Jordenson. Now, it's late. I'll show you to your room."

"I can find my own way, thank you." Eva hurried to the door with a quick "good night" over her shoulder, and made her way down the hall to the stairway.

Once safely in her room, she leaned back against the closed door to catch her breath. What an extraordinary man, she had to admit. To have the capacity for such tenderness, such sensuality yet such extreme violence within one body. Even through the remnants of anger she had to admire his finer qualities. *If only,* she pondered—*if only, what?* She stopped herself. If only, what? What could she be thinking of? As she had told him so convincingly, she was here for the experience of the expedition and nothing else. She had to believe that!

Looking around the room, now lit by a simple but lovely hand-crafted ceramic lamp mounted on the wall at the head of the bed, Eva noticed her bags, which had been neatly placed beside the low table. She also saw that fresh water now filled the pitcher, and fresh towels awaited her use. The bed had been turned back and the pillows fluffed. Eva smiled; Maria had certainly been at work, angel that she was.

Quickly she undressed, washed up, and put on a simple pale blue nightgown, sleeveless, scoop-necked, and knee-length. How inappropriate it was here, she mused. The window had been lowered against the cool night air, so Eva needed no further covering as she sorted through the clothes in her bag, making a small pile of those to pack in her knapsack. Her knapsack! She had left it downstairs! With a groan she realized that she would have to return to the kitchen to get it, preferably without alerting Roberto to her stupidity.

A sharp knock resounded on the hard wood door. Assuming it to be one of two people, she slowly opened it a crack, cautiously peering out while keeping herself hidden behind it. Roberto stood in the hall, her knapsack in one hand, her eyeglasses—had she really forgotten those, too?—in the other.

"You'll be needing these, I believe." His eyes did not stray from hers, or so she thought, as she timidly reached with one hand through the door's narrow opening for the things he held.

"Let me help you." He ignored her outstretched arm, pushing his way into the room before she knew what was happening. He dropped the two items on the bed, then turned toward Eva, whose hand was still on the doorknob, now trembling slightly with indignation. Barefooted as she was, it was a long way up to Roberto's eyes, and she became acutely aware of his towering frame before her. She controlled her voice as she began quietly.

"Thank you for bringing my things up. Now, would you please leave? I have packing to do." The imploring look in her eyes brought him several steps closer. Eva suffered renewed humiliation as his eyes scored her length, taking in the soft curve of her breast and the outline of her waist and hips through the thin material of her shift. Lifting one hand, he slipped his fingers under the lace-edged shoulder strap, sampling the material with the inside of his fingers as their backs gently touched her skin. An electrifying shudder reverberated through her, as she fought back against the reactions she seemed powerless to control. But it seemed her fears were premature.

"Nice," he drawled huskily, before his eyes returned to hers and his tone became suddenly menacing, "but don't bring it tomorrow." It was a command, not a request. And with it he was gone. Eva stood stunned at the open door for several minutes, before she composed herself enough to shut it.

Aware that sleep would be a long time coming that night, she painstakingly went over and over her suitcase, choosing the few items she thought most appropriate to bring. Once decided, she then found that only half of them fit into the knapsack, so she began the process of elimination all over again. She finally settled on two pairs of blue jeans, one to wear and one to pack, several T-shirts, the necessary underthings, and a heavy pullover sweater. For want of something better, she would wear sneakers, though she had to admit that Paul's arguments in favor of hiking boots made sense. *Water over the dam,* she sighed, as she stowed a towel, soap, and the minimum of makeup needs into the pack.

Standing back, she realized that there was no way she could get any camera equipment into the knapsack. Knowing full well that she risked Roberto's wrath, she proceeded to repack the duffel that usually held her camera equipment. She would need everything in it— her tripod film, flash, lenses, and various accessories— at one point or another, though she would keep the camera itself around her neck. She was able to eliminate only the film she had already exposed. Taking a deep breath, she prayed that the case wouldn't really be all that noticeable. It had a broad shoulder strap, and she was well used to carrying it. This crucial decision having been made, she put everything else back into her large suitcase, turned out the light, and climbed into bed.

Even then, she lay awake for what seemed to be hours. As her mind reviewed the amazing events of the day, she momentarily relived each of the experiences and their emotions. Perhaps it was this past excitement, perhaps it was anticipation of tomorrow, perhaps it was no more than the *cafèzinho,* which had keyed her up. When exhaustion finally engulfed her, she fell into a deep and dreamless sleep.

It seemed mere moments later that Eva felt a movement at her shoulder. Shrugging it off, she turned deeper into the pillow . . . before bolting upright in alarm at the sudden realization of where she was and that there was someone with her. In the faint bluish light which was quickly replacing the dark of the night, she saw Roberto sitting on the edge of the bed.

"You startled me!" she gasped breathlessly, trying to get her bearings amid the lingering grogginess.

He nodded understandably, his hand remaining on her shoulder for a minute too long, and he informed her in a low tone, "It's time to get up. Maria will have breakfast ready in five minutes." Then, mercifully, he left the room without another word, permitting her the privacy to dress.

Breakfast was a quiet, peaceful affair, as Eva readily let her persisting drowsiness cushion her. She felt in no rush to completely wake up, and rather enjoyed the eggs and bacon from her semidazed state. Roberto was faintly amused by her condition, though he made no effort to alter it. He talked periodically to Maria in low, fluent Portuguese, relieving Eva of any responsibility for conversation. Whenever Maria passed behind Eva in the course of her work, she put a gently reassuring hand on the latter's shoulder; Eva returned the gesture with a smile, grateful for the comfort as well as for the most satisfying breakfast. When Eva did occasionally raise her eyes to Roberto over the rim of her coffee cup, she encountered a pleasant, if impersonal, expression. Even through her stupor she guessed that it was the impending embarkation that had put him in relatively good humor.

It was only when breakfast was done and the two passed through the living room to pick up their packs that this good humor was tested. As Eva bent to lift her two bags, the knapsack and the duffel, Roberto's gaze caught the latter. With a flicker of impatience in his eyes he faced her.

"I said you could bring only one bag. You have two."

Eva had prepared herself well the night before and now, fully awake, she advanced her case.

"I only have one—my knapsack. This duffel holds the tools of my trade much as your pack donkeys carry the tools of yours. I'm used to carrying it and can easily handle both. Without this duffel, my whole purpose for this trip is lost. And I can't very well leave the few clothes in my knapsack behind, can I?"

She had psyched him out perfectly, she knew, as she silently congratulated herself. Although her touch of humor at the end had caused him to raise a suggestive eyebrow, he had responded to reasoning as she had somehow known he would. Instinct told her that this man was a level-headed businessman, steady, practical and straightforward; it was only in his personal affairs, she winced, that he was so unpredictable.

Conceding defeat, he shrugged. "They're your shoulders," he grumbled, half to himself, as he led the way out of the house.

The early morning sky was the palest shade of blue, a bare suggestion of things to come; the sun, not yet clearing the mountains, painted a thin golden line across the eastern ridge. Eva followed Roberto down the cobblestoned streets, her sneakers a vast improvement on the high-heeled sandals she had worn yesterday. They turned this way and that, passing from one street into another. Roberto walked several paces ahead and didn't look back to check that she kept up.

Eva was surprised by the amount of activity already underway in the small village at such an ungodly hour. Each man and woman they passed greeted Roberto enthusiastically, and he returned each salutation with a warm comment, often a personal acknowledgment. He was both well known and well liked here, Eva concluded, and he seemed in his element as he moved through the narrow streets.

Just as Eva began to wonder whether there really was a point of departure, they turned a corner into an enclosed square, and in the center were gathered the remaining members of the group, the donkeys Roberto had promised, and a short and swarthy man similar in appearance to so many of those she had seen yesterday from the taxi. Numerous boxes, bedrolls, canvas-wrapped tools and other utensils were anchored securely atop each donkey. Eva wondered if this packing had been Roberto's handiwork; he looked so fresh and alert, she couldn't imagine his having been up for several hours already, whereas the small Brazilian, as agreeable as he appeared, did show some signs of wear and tear. Eva suspected, smiling, that given a choice he would be standing over another *cafèzinho* with his compatriots.

Paul and Tom broke away from the group and came forward to meet them as they approached, Tom reaching gallantly to relieve Eva of the duffel. She turned down his offer firmly, insisting that she could handle the heavy bag, then she stole a triumphant glance at Roberto. Her gesture had been wasted; the latter was occupied rechecking the donkeys as he talked with the Brazilian. Quickly erasing any signs of disappointment, Eva turned to greet the others, Jacques and Pierre, both of whom appeared rested and enthusiastic, though Pierre was unable to totally disguise the brooding look that she found so disquieting.

As they awaited Roberto's word to set off, Eva stepped back from the others and began to take pictures. Determined to keep a running photographic narrative of the expedition, she made snaps of the square in which they gathered, including the donkeys with their packs, the pile of knapsacks on the pavement waiting to be hoisted onto the appropriate backs, the little Brazilian at work with Roberto, tightening the cinch on one animal, rebalancing the load on another, and the four other men gathered together in friendly conversation. Past experience had taught Eva to expect some early self-consciousness and awkwardness in her subjects. These subjects didn't disappoint her. Roberto and the Brazilian had been too preoccupied to even notice her, much to her relief; the other men were a different story. Of the four, only Jacques took her activities in stride. Paul and Tom, God bless them, immediately took to hamming it up, facing the lens head-on with ear-to-ear grins on their faces and arms across each other's shoulders. They could have been posing high atop Mt. Everest, thought Eva with a snicker, for the look of triumph they mockingly wore. Their awareness of the camera didn't faze her in the least, for she knew that they would soon become oblivious to it. She had to admit that the pictures she had just shot would capture some truth about their subjects—Paul and Tom were nuts, lovable nuts! She rather enjoyed their antics, particularly as they buoyed her to take several shots of the malevolent-looking Pierre, his glare zeroing through the lens at her.

When the last of the details had been seen to, Roberto gave the sign, and they were off. Eva couldn't help but share the excitement of the others. The expedition promised to be a rare experience and was certainly a far cry from anything she had ever done before. She suddenly realized that this trip was already doing its job; even through yesterday's emotional upheavals, she had brooded less about Stu, their failed marriage, and her widowhood than she'd done in a fortnight. Even with as little sleep as she had had last night, she felt exhilarated, and her step increased as she took her place in the small procession.

They passed out of the square as they had entered it, then turned onto the cobblestoned street heading away from the center of town, if in fact that was what the close cluster of houses was called. The sun had now risen above the hills, its warming glow intermingling with the surface chill of the stones. An occasional villager passed the group in the opposite direction, an occasional head nodded at a window, an occasional hand waved its greeting of farewell and luck. Within a few minutes the clop-clop of the donkeys' hooves ceased as the cobblestones gave way to dirt and the town was left behind.

Talk was practically nonexistent during this exit. Eva suspected that, like herself, each of the group was savoring the peace of the morning, reveling in the inner excitement, perhaps daydreaming as to where the hike would lead. She felt all these things and more. Although Roberto was well ahead of her, she was acutely aware of him. He looked so masculine, damn him, in his snug-fitting denims and his tapered shirt. His pace was strong, his stance erect and confident, knapsack and all. The wide-brimmed hat was in place once again, warding off any stray rays of the sun.

In between her thoughts Eva continued to photograph. She captured the town as it disappeared behind them; she captured the dull green foliage on either side of the trail; she captured the distant hills above them, dotted wth small pockets of mist, the last remnants of a wayward cloud. The path they walked on was narrow, allowing no more than two abreast. Once leaving the town, it became a slow but steady climb, the gradual gain in altitude demanding little from the hikers. Very pleasant, thought Eva, as she shifted her shoulder straps and adjusted her stride to keep pace with the others.

They plodded along thus for several hours. With the sun higher in the sky, the heat increased, adding to the natural warmth of exertion. Eva's shoulders indeed began to ache—score one for Roberto, she lamented—but her feet were doing just fine. Score one for sneakers, she came back triumphantly. Just then Paul dropped back from his position directly behind Roberto. Was he checking up on her or just visiting?

"How're you doin', kid?" he asked, in the warm and sincere manner that had immediately endeared him to her.

"Great! How about you?" she returned, not quite honestly, but hoping that he would talk with her awhile and perhaps take her mind off her aching shoulders. Much to her pleasure, that seemed to have been his intention, so they moved along side by side for a while. The group, though otherwise in single file, had spread out significantly, with Roberto in the lead and the donkeys in the rear. This distance put Eva and Paul out of earshot of the others, so she felt totally relaxed in the conversation.

"Tell me about yourself, Paul," she asked with genuine interest.

"Well, ah, let me see." The consummate joker, he rolled his eyes upward, squinting as he did so, as though he had so many, many years to dig from and couldn't quite decide where to begin.

"I was born in New York, though we moved to Chicago when I was three, so I don't remember much. My dad worked for a national insurance company and was periodically transferred. We lived in a huge high-rise in Chicago until I was seven, when we moved to Boston. My mother still lives there, in an apartment overlooking the Charles River." He paused, temporarily lost in thought. *So that was why Roberto spent so much time in Boston,* she reasoned, *with his mother still there!*

"Your father?" she redirected him.

"He died. Four years ago, now. It was very hard on my mother. They were so close. And his death was very sudden. Roberto was a great help—" he stopped abruptly, wondering if he had spilled the beans.

Eva laughed aloud at his guilty look, the laugh loosening the tension in her shoulders as her feet plodded on. "I know. Roberto told me last night."

"What else did Roberto tell you last night?" A mischievous gleam in his eye, Paul had lowered his voice to one of mocking intimacy.

Eva blushed. "I mean, I guessed the relationship and Roberto confirmed it. The resemblance is remarkable."

Becoming serious again, Paul continued his earlier thought. "Roberto was terrific. He helped my mother over a rough time and me as well. I don't have any other siblings. Roberto became a real brother to me."

"Hadn't you known him before that?"

"Oh, yes. He spent several months a year, mostly vacations, with us from the earliest time I can remember. But we were never very close. He was a thorn in my father's side. And my father, at his best, was no easy man to get along with! My mother is a saint to have loved him so." He smiled in resignation, sadness again pervading his recollections.

"What about Roberto? Did he spend the rest of his time in Brazil?" Subconsciously, Eva had narrowed the conversation.

Paul looked at his boots, keeping the gentle pace of the hike, the dust of the path beginning to dull their sheen. *He seems hesitant to say too much about Roberto*, thought Eva. *Almost protective.* After several minutes, having evidently resolved some internal dilemma, he replied to her questions.

"Roberto spent most of his time in the States, either at boarding school or on vacation with us. Although his home was formally in São Paulo with his father, he didn't spend much time there until he had graduated from business school and returned there to live. Then we didn't see him as often. Mother missed him."

Eva's own maternal instinct must have been pricked. "Wouldn't he have been better off with his mother than at boarding school?" Then realizing the ramifications, she added, "Oh, I'm sorry. It's really none of my business."

"That's okay. You have to understand Brazilian values, Eva," he replied patiently. "Education is an important source of status. Although Roberto's father was well established, he wanted to guarantee everything for his son, particularly since . . ." Here he stopped, knowing he had almost gone too far. *Since what?* Eva's curiosity had been aroused. She had taken in every bit of the information he had given her about Roberto, in hopes that it would help her better understand this enigmatic man. *What was this last hesitation?* Paul interrupted her thoughts.

"And speaking of the man, I'd better go up and see how we're doing. Talk with you later, Eva!"

Where he got the energy to sprint ahead to where Roberto was steadily plodding, she would never know. She had enjoyed their conversation but now was becoming uncomfortably aware of muscles, everywhere, declaring their existence. And she thought she had been in such good shape, always on the go at work! Well, she rationalized, as long as she could keep her moans and groans to herself. She would not give Roberto the satisfaction of discovering her weakness.

Mercifully, the group soon stopped for a rest and some lunch. Eva busied herself with her camera bag as she sat on the hard ground, its sparse covering of grass no cushion, though even its bumps were a welcome relief to Eva, having now removed the weight from both her shoulders and her feet. She avoided Roberto's gaze as he passed her on his way to the donkeys. When he returned he carried two small paper sacks, one of which he dropped in her lap as he squatted down in front of her, his back to the others. His face was expressionless, but his dark eyes bore through her and his tone was cold.

"How are you holding up?"

"Just fine! I'm sorry to disappoint you!" Eva shot back, a bit too defensively. A slow smile played on his thin lips, a faint light twinkled from the depths of his black eyes in amusement at her reflex.

"Just wondering. I don't want any lame animals, human or otherwise, this trip," he murmured, as he straightened up and headed toward the others. "Help yourself! Lunch is over with Carlos!" he called to the others, once again letting his tongue play in a strictly Brazilian way with the pronunciation of the native's name. Turning a final time toward Eva in silent conveyance of a subtle message of understanding, he deposited himself on the ground and concentrated on his own lunch.

Eva frowned in self-disgust. How could she be so transparent? He seemed to know her as well as she knew herself. She contemplated getting up and moving around, anywhere, just to prove his assumptions wrong, but she didn't quite trust her leg muscles yet and she wanted every minute of rest that he would permit. Instead, she settled for a scowl of defiance sent in his direction, before she turned to her own refreshment.

Tom had settled himself near Eva and kept up a steady train of chatter, which she found to be both diverting and enjoyable. Once her eye skirted the group and came inadvertently to rest on Roberto's, instantly locking into the intense concentration of his gaze. She was mesmerized by him. His eyes gripped and held her just as his hands had done on other occasions. But she could read nothing in them, nor did she try. His mastery over her frightened her, yet she was powerless to tear her gaze from his. When he finally diverted his eyes, thereby releasing her, she jerked her gaze back to Tom self-consciously; the latter was unable to hide, in his running commentary, a hint of embarrassment at the visual possession he had witnessed. Eva politely listened to, though heard very little of, Tom's remaining chatter; she responded when appropriate but knew her mind dwelled on Roberto.

He had, she acknowledged unwillingly, become an increasing presence in her thoughts. There was so much about him that puzzled her. She knew so little of him, yet they shared an intimacy in every glance. He seemed to know her mind, anticipating her inner thoughts and actions. And as much as she fought him, she knew that in the end she would have to yield to him, as much of her own volition as his.

CHAPTER 5

The rest stop was over and the line of march resumed. Eva had been rejuvenated by the break, her muscles regaining some of their strength. She knew that although they would be a lot sorer by nightfall, they had to become accustomed to the steady pace sooner or later. While still fresh from the brief hiatus, she worked with her camera, as much as the uninterrupted movement of the caravan would allow. The view changed subtly as they gradually gained altitude; she photographed these new vistas and the foliage of the mountainside, so far from being lush, yet so beautiful in its ruggedness.

The midday sun had begun to leave its mark. Sweat trickled from Eva's scalp, down her neck, gathering in the bend of her elbows as they folded to allow her moist palms to ease the burden of the shoulder straps. Beneath the knapsack her T-shirt clung to her. Perspiration dotted her midriff where her camera bag occasionally made contact.

The men were not immune to the heat either, much to Eva's satisfaction. The Frenchmen, walking abreast now and exchanging words in their native tongue, had slowed some, falling back nearer to Eva. Tom, to her amusement, gesticulated periodically with his hands, fanning his face, flapping his wings, all in an attempt to cool himself and well aware that he was on a stage entertaining those behind him. Paul, further ahead, kept up the pace diligently, his only sign of discomfort the occasional mopping of his forehead with the back of his hand.

Roberto, on whose striding form Eva's eyes eventually fell, seemed barely aware of the sun's searing rays. The band of his hat had taken on the darker hue of moisture and his forearms glistened faintly with sweat as they swung gently at his sides, but otherwise he seemed to be thoroughly enjoying both the weather and the physical exertion. *His composure is unfair,* she thought maddeningly, looking again to the others for justification of her own discomfort.

Through the afternoon they moved onward, the overall speed slowing somewhat as Roberto geared his pace to the majority. The climb was neither straight nor steadily up, now. The small troop wound its way on the worn path that clung to the mountainside, mounting the top of a ridge then descending in its wake. Along the downward stretches Eva felt herself propelled along by sheer force of gravity; her legs by now were taking very few directions from her brain.

The worst of the heat climaxed at midafternoon, and soon the sun moved further across the sky to throw the group mercifully into the bright, but more bearable by far, shadow of the hill they hugged.

Eva pushed herself on and on, her shoulders now numb under their punishing weights and her feet beyond the point of sensation. Under the command of anyone else she would have begged for more rest along the way, but under Roberto's lead it was another matter. He was intent on reaching the deserted mine by midday tomorrow, which meant a minimum of stops today. When he finally did signal an end to the day's climb, Eva saw that they were at a larger clearing than the mere hints of ones they had paused at earlier. Roberto knew the route well. This clearing must have been the day's goal all along, and he had succeeded in pushing each and every one of them to his limit to reach it. Begrudgingly, Eva had to admire his perseverance, even as her muscles throbbed in disagreement.

The clearing was just off the main path, large enough to accommodate the whole group and open enough to permit a small fire without danger of conflagration. Eva lowered her packs at the base of a stunted tree, much like the others rimming the clearing. Impulsively, she collapsed onto her back, knees bent, arm across her eyes, where she lay in pure exhaustion, heedless of any activity that might be taking place around her.

In fact, there was practically none. The others, as tired as she, had adopted similar poses; each kept to himself as though centering every bit of psychic energy on the thought of rest and relaxation. Only Roberto and Carlos kept busy, tying the donkeys securely and unloading the packs. At one point Roberto called on Jacques to give him a hand, but he seemed otherwise content to work himself.

Just as Eva's breathing began to settle down to a more even beat, she heard footsteps close beside her ear. Removing her arm from across her eyes and squinting up into the shadow looming over her, she saw Roberto and the faint amusement in his grin.

"Rested?" he taunted, knowing full well that it would be a long time before she would be able to answer that honestly.

"Of course!" she jumped up, wincing involuntarily at the pain in her thighs at the sudden movement.

"What can I do?" she asked impatiently, seeking to compensate for the grimace, which she was sure he had seen and obviously enjoyed.

He set her to work unloading the cooking utensils, while he doled out chores to the others. When she had completed this, he ushered her to the pack containing their dinner, with instructions on how to prepare it.

"When Paul has finished building the fire, you can start to cook. I'll leave that to you. I'm sure you've had more experience at it than we have," he mocked her, the gleam of his white teeth showing through his satanic grin.

Eva glared at him as she set to work. It wasn't the work she objected to, she knew, but rather his attitude toward her. He was purposely pushing her hard out of spite; he was determined to see her crumble in the face of the challenge. Well, she would not let that happen! Her own anger and rising determination gave her the strength she needed to prepare the dinner, which at any other time she would have thoroughly enjoyed doing.

Paul started a good fire and Eva managed to improvise with the cooking equipment the simple grilling of the steaks which had been supplied. The other men, having completed their own jobs by now, talked among themselves while she worked. Only Roberto seemed somewhat aloof, leaning lazily against a tree on the outskirts of the group. Whether he was watching her she couldn't tell, though she stole a sideways glance at him from time to time. It must have been her comment the evening before about "woman's work" that had prompted this punishment of her, she concluded. *I'll show him I can cope with this and more,* she vowed under her breath, accidentally burning her finger on a pot handle, then rushing it to her mouth to ease the pain.

Fortunately the meal went well, despite the throbbing finger which now joined Eva's muscles in rebellion. The men, with the exception of Roberto, complimented her profusely for the delicious fare, appreciative of the toll her work must have taken on her exhausted body.

As they ate, the conversation revolved around their anticipated arrival the next day at the deserted mine, where the Espinhaco Topaz was last seen.

"Where did you find that map, Roberto? Have you ever been up here before?" Tom's enthusiasm was infectious.

"The map belonged to an old man who lived in Terra Vermelho. I had known him well as a child, since I spent much time here. When he died last year he left the map for me, knowing of my interest in such adventures. No, I've never been to this mine before, though I've traveled through the Serra do Espinhaco many times. I used to guide groups of visiting explorers, thus the old man knew of my passion!" Here he looked at Eva, the double meaning thick on his tongue.

Eva looked away quickly, hoping that none of the others would catch the suggestion. Jacques now picked up the train of conversation, his accent lending an air of romance to the expedition.

"Why has the old mine been unexplored for so long? Did no one try to find the Topaz before?"

Roberto was prepared for this query, as he continued his narrative. "The native Brazilians hold many superstitions, one relating to a primitive creature, half man and half beast, who wanders the Serra do Espinhaco. The map has been passed on for three generations, each one either fearing to search for the Topaz or unable to organize an expedition. I am not a superstitious man, though I would advise you not to wander too far from camp tonight." He finished with a sly, almost demonic smile; in that instant Eva could have believed this man to be related to the legendary creature.

Eva had been sitting with the others in relaxed formation around the glowing embers of the fire. The air was comfortable now, devoid of chill yet a sharp contrast to the day's heat. It entered her mind to photograph this intimate and friendly gathering, but the thought of disturbing her weary bones was too painful. She had, as it was, removed her sneakers to expose the raw blisters on each heel to the soothing air. Now she opted for pure relaxation, joining the discussion as she found it becoming more and more fascinating.

"What will we find, exactly, when we get to the mine, Roberto?" she asked, unconsciously batting at the small insects which, attracted by the light of the dying fire, swarmed about.

"That I can't tell you. I've had to guess as to what equipment to bring. At best we'll find the entrance to the mine and its long corridors open. My map directs us from the top, so we won't get lost once inside the mine. It could be easy sailing all the way, right to the ledge on which the Topaz supposedly sits."

"And at worst?" interjected Pierre, the pessimist always.

Roberto turned toward him, his expression growing more serious now. "At worst we'll find the mine collapsed—shafts, entrance, everything. We have some digging equipment if it's just the case of one corridor or another being blocked. Also, if it's just the entrance, we can probably dig through. But if it's the works, then it would take many more days than we have supplies for and much heavier equipment than ours to extricate the Topaz. In that case, our little jaunt will have been in vain, at least in regard to the Espinhaco Topaz." His sad smile echoed Eva's sentiments, although she was beginning to wonder if the Topaz would indeed be the greatest memory of this trip for her. Her own sad smile turned to Roberto, and in that moment she knew that when she returned to New York the memory of him would probably outlive that of the Topaz. For in his strangely quixotic way he had awakened feelings within her that she thought to be long dead. He had made her feel alive again, at times gloriously and at times regretfully, but nonetheless alive!

What insanity, she scolded herself! What was she thinking about this Roberto de Carvalho? Women were his specialty—charm them, seduce them, then desert them. She wouldn't let herself fall into that trap. But she was jumping the gun, wasn't she? He despised her as much as she wanted to despise him. He thought she was some cheap tramp, a sex-starved black widow, he had called her. She'd have to keep her distance, she warned herself once more. She couldn't trust him, and she feared increasingly that she couldn't trust herself.

"You look so sad, Eva. Does the prospect of seeing the Espinhaco Topaz mean so much to you?" Roberto's mocking tone broke into her thoughts, causing a blush to creep up from her neck camouflaged only by the fading light of dusk.

Her head jerked toward him. "Ah . . . no . . . I mean, what a shame it would be to have come all this way and be thwarted by nature itself! What could cause a collapse of the mine? Are there earthquakes around here?"

"No. No earthquakes. No blizzards. Just rain. Not very often. Not very long. But when it comes it hits hard. Torrents. Over the years a few such torrential downpours could have gradually weakened the structure enough to have caused a cave-in."

"But when was the last time the mine has been seen . . . open?" Tom broke in.

"A group of Canadian hikers scored the Serra do

Espinhaco four years ago," Roberto replied. "Although they were mainly here for the hiking, one of them was an historian doing a dissertation on the Brazilian gold rush and its profound effects on the country. As they hiked, he mapped each of the paths they covered, labeling the location of each of the mines and its condition. When I came into possession of this map, I contacted him and he confirmed that four years ago this mine entrance was open. I would have come soon after I got the map, but I had neither the time nor the company then. As I said, none of the natives want to come up here. Fortunately for us, Carlos is beyond superstition. And he needs the money!" He smiled warmly as he looked toward Carlos, who sat apart from the core of the group as though he were more comfortable with the donkeys. At the mention of his name he raised a hand in recognition of the only word he could understand. Roberto said something briefly to him in Portuguese, then turned back to the fire.

Remembering the early start they had made that morning, Eva ventured timidly, "What time are we starting out tomorrow?" She immediately regretted the question, as Roberto's gaze became one of derision.

"I'd like to be off by sunup again, so we can reach the mine by early afternoon, before the worst of the heat sets in. Can you make it?" he aimed his question solely at Eva.

"I did it this morning, didn't I?" she retorted, trying to disguise her annoyance in front of the others.

He continued to provoke her. "I think you'd better begin cleaning up these plates and pans if you want to get much rest tonight!"

Of all the nerve, simmered Eva. *I make the meal, tired as I am, and he thinks I'm just going to abide by his command and clean up, too? We'll see who commands here!* Her indignant reply raised all heads.

"I have no intention of waiting on any of you. If anyone here wants to eat food cooked on clean pans off clean plates tomorrow, you'd better get off your butts and help!" She was furious with Roberto, though she tried to add a note of humor for the sake of the others. With that, she rose and moved toward the fire, tossing instructions here and there as she went, though sparing Roberto a direct order. She had no desire to test his compliance, or to work side by side with him, for that matter!

Paul and Tom were quick to help her, and the three of them had everything cleaned in no time. Meanwhile, Roberto and the two Frenchmen sorted out bedrolls from the rest of the supplies.

Eva was still bristling from Roberto's put-down when the last of the utensils had been stowed away for the night. Paul, particularly aware of her annoyance, tried to coax her into a better mood.

"Come and sit with us awhile, Eva. It's still early. I'd like to hear more about your work."

But Eva doubted she would be fit company for anyone in her agitated state, overreaction that she knew it was. "Thanks, Paul. You're a sweetheart. But I think I'd like a little time to myself," she gently refused, needing time to cool off.

Turning, she slowly wandered toward the edge of the clearing, padding carefully, barefooted as she was. She paused at a secluded corner, hidden from the rest by low shrubbery and the rocky bulge of the mountainside, where she sat down cross-legged to stare out at the skyline. The moon had risen and cast its silvery glow over the landscape. From the vantage point of her private niche, she could see for miles, the craggy mountains and furrowed valleys below her such a contrasting sight to the view from her New York town house. Funny, she thought, there's not a soul out there in the mountains, yet I don't feel any of the loneliness I feel in New York looking out over millions of people! There was a certain peacefulness, a oneness with nature which now eased her muscles as no Jacuzzi could. She felt the tension gradually flowing from her body out over the valleys, to be swallowed up forever beyond the farthest mountain top.

Entranced by the vista, Eva was oblivious to all sounds around her. She jumped in surprise at the hand that lay on her shoulder, reflexively jerking her body away from its grasp. Instantly she recognized her companion, no longer needing to see his face to know of his presence. Her senses had memorized his very smell, so fresh and masculine and heady. There was a moment's hesitation before Roberto's voice, low and gruff, shattered the silence.

"Let me see your finger," he ordered, grabbing the forefinger of her right hand before she understood what he was doing.

"Ouch . . . watch it!" she exclaimed, his hand having grazed the very spot she had burned earlier. He had taken a small tube from his shirt pocket and was proceeding to spread, none too gently for Eva's comfort, a salve on the burn which, though small, had begun to blister.

"I didn't think you'd noticed," Eva shot at him sarcastically, even as the soothing effect of the salve had begun to ease the sting.

"I don't miss too much." His eyes didn't stray from hers, the implication of his tone notwithstanding. "Here . . . you'll need these for tomorrow. You can't very well hike barefoot over the hills. And, as I said once before, I won't have any lame animals along." Reaching again into the pocket of his shirt, he drew out several Band-Aids, obviously intended for her raw heels.

By this time Eva's humiliation had nowhere to go.

Once again he was right. As much as she would have liked to turn down his smug gesture of help, she knew she would need the bandages if she ever hoped to put her sneakers on. Betrayed by her feet, she burst out in a spontaneous eruption of laughter at the ludicrous predicament.

"I'm glad to see your humor has returned. I thought for a while, there, that we'd seen the last of it! It becomes you." He stated it as a fact, but there was a gentleness in his voice.

"If you like it so much, why do you constantly provoke me? You do, you know." She stated her own fact, calmly.

"I didn't say I like it. I merely said it becomes you. There is a difference. And if I provoke you it's because you are oversensitive. I enjoy your outbursts of anger. They also become you, in their own way." Roberto's gentle tone was causing flutters within her, even as his words angered her.

"So you enjoy annoying me!" she retorted. "What kind of perverted mind can do that? You must be a sadist. You humiliate me, hurt me, tease me, infuriate me . . . and love every minute of it! What does make you tick? I'm at a total loss to figure you out!"

His expression softened, pleased to hear her admit to a weakness. "Well, I'm glad to see there's something you're at a loss to do. You are pretty self-sufficient, I have to admit. What makes *you* tick, Mrs. Jordenson?"

"Uh-uh. I asked you first." Eva was not about to be put off when she was so close to a real discovery. "You must have a very low opinion of women."

"To the contrary. I have the utmost respect for some women."

"Then you must despise American women." She pursued the point, eager to pin him down somehow.

"Not at all. My mother is an American woman." He

was evading her questions, and Eva knew she would have to be more specific.

"Your mother doesn't count. Are you married?" She dove in headfirst, not sure whether she would hit bottom or rise to the surface.

"No," he replied bluntly. "Do I seem like the marrying type?"

"No. Ah, yes! I would have guessed that you weren't married but that you would like to be and to have a family." Eva was talking freely now, saying things which at another time she might not have ventured to say. But Roberto's seemingly relaxed mood gave her courage.

An enigmatic smile curled at the corners of his mouth, a mixture of sadness and frustration. "You know all the answers, don't you? How did you reach that conclusion?"

"The way you look at Paul and talk about him. It's something special, isn't it? I don't have any brothers or sisters, but I would have liked to feel about one the way you seem to feel about Paul. And I imagine that feeling would be magnified with your own children. I know . . ." she broke off, having unconsciously broached a subject she didn't want to discuss.

Roberto, as was becoming his way, immediately picked up on it. "You know, what?" He paused, his eyes registering surprise at a completely new thought. "Do you have any children, Eva?"

Eva's gaze had returned to the distant mountains, though her mind's eye saw the skyscrapers of the city. She answered softly, sadness overhanging her words. "No. I don't have any children. I was . . . pregnant once . . . but I lost the baby."

There was silence for several moments until Roberto genuinely touched by her sadness, broke it. "It must have been very painful for you?" he asked, urging her to talk of the experience for the cathartic value of airing it.

"It was. Very painful. I never talk of it. I never think of it." The factuality in Eva's voice wouldn't hide completely the suffering she felt at the reminder of this very personal tragedy. Why it flowed to the surface now, after months and months of total denial, Eva didn't know. Some force, powerful and intimate, though silent, gently coaxed her on.

"Soon after Stu and I married, I discovered I was pregnant. Stu didn't want the baby; it wouldn't fit in with his life-style. I did want the child. I had no family and desperately wanted some blood tie." Her eyes hadn't strayed from the mountains. Quickly she continued. "I loved being pregnant. Such a beautiful, natural feeling, as though I was doing what my body was meant to do, pure and simple." Here she did venture to smile at Roberto, shyly, suddenly embarrassed by her confession but knowing she was helpless to halt it. His expression was somber, frightening her into a hasty summing up.

"At any rate, I lost the baby at four months. Not very long. But I'll always remember that feeling . . ." Her voice trailed off toward the mountains she faced. Taking a deep breath, she added, "I can imagine the intensity of love you'll feel for your children someday."

Again, a silence. Then his soothing voice probed further. "Certainly you'll have other children someday?"

Bitterness tinged her brief laugh as she scolded, "I'm a widow, remember? You keep reminding me of that fact. And as such it would be difficult for me to have any children. Am I right? Contrary to your belief, I am neither in the market for a husband nor a father for any potential children."

Roberto seemed momentarily lost in his own reveries. "You'd make a good mother . . . although I pity the poor husband you snag someday," he teased once more.

"Fortunately that's none of your affair. Anyway, marriage is the last thing that is on my mind. My husband is not yet dead a month! You must think me some flighty fortune hunter!" Eva exploded, half in reaction to his words and half in regret at the loss of the moment of tenderness he had shown.

"Take it easy! Take it easy!" he crooned softly. "You're very touchy tonight. It must be the hard day you've had," he added, smirking in the moonlight.

Eva would not be placated. "If I've had a hard day, it's mostly your fault. Now, if you'll excuse me, I think I'll turn in." She had let him provoke her again, she realized, as she stood up in a huff and whirled around to return to the fire.

"Acch . . ." a groan escaped, involuntarily, as Eva felt a muscle spasm at the sudden movement.

"Here, let me help you," Roberto ordered, firmly grabbing her arm and returning her to her position overlooking the outstretched valley. Before she could protest, his hands had begun a gentle massage of her aching shoulders, the instantaneous comfort silencing any argument she might have made.

"Relax," he commanded softly, his hands continuing to knead her battered muscles. Whether it was the stroking motion of his hands or the mere physical closeness of him, Eva let herself unwind, dropping her chin onto her chest with a sigh of pleasure. Gently his hands moved to her arms, caressing her smooth skin below the sleeve of her T-shirt. She couldn't even object when they slipped inside the neckline of her shirt to rub the bare skin of her lower neck and shoulders. She stood, eyes closed, head down, hypnotized by his touch, tingling under his fingertips. She was not aware when the fine line was crossed between physical therapy and seduction, but she didn't fight him when he raised his hand to her long curls, lifting them enough to allow his lips to play on the back of her neck. She swayed, then moaned aloud, this time of a more erotic pleasure, as he drew her slim body back against the masculine contours of his. Her head fell back against his chest as he wrapped his arms around her midriff. It was as though she floated in a never-never land of ecstasy, losing all touch with reality. Her own compelling need made her turn around to face him, her arms slowly creeping up his chest, reveling in the firmness of his taut muscles.

Her eyes were frozen on his lips, as his were on hers. It was a sensuous exchange, so near yet not touching. His hands explored the hollows of her back, the line of her spine, the curve of her hips, as he pressed her arching body firmly against his. Eva felt his male need, in turn igniting a treacherous sensation in the pit of her stomach. No longer able to keep any distance, she parted her lips and raised herself to meet his in a kiss of frenzied passion and overwhelming need. His demanding lips caressed hers, his tongue probing the recesses of her mouth.

Her trembling limbs clung to him, arms wrapped tightly around his neck, locking herself into his embrace. It was a short distance for him to reach to her knees and sweep her, weightless, into his arms, without the slightest disruption of their passion-devouring kiss.

Eva moaned softly as he lay her down on a grassy spot against the rocky wall nearby. "Your muscles?" he asked, fearing that he had hurt her.

"No, yours," she murmured breathlessly. "What is it you do to me?" she pleaded, burying her hands in his thick hair and drawing his face down to hers in renewed embrace. His body moved to partially cover hers, his hands beginning a lust-arousing exploration of her flesh. Her T-shirt was no barrier as his fingers delved beneath to touch the bare skin of her midriff, sending flames of excitement through her as a prelude to the greater ardor as they moved up to circle the swell of her breast.

Eva had never known the height of passion to which his spell now drew her, rising higher and higher with each caress, each soul-reaching kiss. Her nostrils gloried in his smell, her hands in the feel of his strong flesh beneath her searching palms. She savored the taste of his lips, smoldering against hers, his tongue seeking out hers. Desire consumed her as her fingers, in trembling haste, unbuttoned his shirt to romp amid the luxuriant blanket on his chest.

His lips left hers to nibble at her ear lobe, her chin, then sear a path down her neck and shoulders to the graceful cleavage between her breasts. Any second thoughts she might have had vanished as he gently eased the scooped neck of her T-shirt aside, followed by the lacy cup of her bra, to expose her cream-colored breast. Explosive currents raced through her as his tongue explored their rosy peaks, firming instantly under his touch. Mercifully, at the moment when she would have cried out in delight, his lips recaptured hers, becoming more demanding as was his own need.

"Oh, my God, I want you so much." The soft whisper had escaped Eva's lips, even as Roberto kissed them into silence.

"Eva? . . . Eva?" Her name filtered through the aura of passion. Roberto's body stiffened as she realized that the lips so close to hers had made no sound. Paul! Looking for her! She tensed in turn, totally immobilized by the shock of the interruption.

Roberto held her to him, tighter if anything, as he called back to Paul in a calm, even voice, "She's with me, Paulo. We'll join you in a couple of minutes." The familiar form of his name took any edge off the reply. They remained as they were, bodies intertwined, the only sound the frantic beating of two hearts amid the crunch of receding footsteps over the dry ground.

Alone once again, Roberto sat up, gently drawing Eva with him before releasing her to move back several feet. The moment was gone; each knew it. Eva felt screams of frustration gathering at the back of her throat. Determined to regain her lost control, she stood up, took several deep breaths, and began to straighten the clothing which had come askew. Roberto did the same, though she saw no sign of any torment he might be suffering as a result of their checked passion.

"That shouldn't have happened. I'm sorry," Eva began tremulously, eyes downcast.

When he made no response she looked up to meet his gaze. No thoughts escaped the murky depths of his black eyes, but the moonlight betrayed a look of measured anger around his mouth. She flinched even before he spoke.

"Make sure it doesn't happen again," he hissed through thin-drawn lips as he pivoted and headed back toward the camp. In spite of her own remonstration, Eva was stunned and hurt by his rejection. It took her several minutes more to compose herself enough to follow him.

Moments later, her bedroll wrapped around her more for psychological protection than climatic, she was engulfed by a wave of misery, an ache of torment she'd never known before. Ironic, she thought bitterly, how she could be so high and then so low within such a short time. What a fool she had made of herself. How could she have betrayed herself so blatantly? This man would wreak havoc within her. He couldn't offer her the stability she wanted, the protection she needed, the love she craved. Then it hit her like a bolt: Love, the word she had avoided in all her thoughts of him. But now she knew; there was no further question in her mind. For every fiber in her body and very soul that warned her against Roberto there was a matching fiber that cried out her love for him. She loved him. As she had never loved before. Desirous only of being with him, sensing him, wanting him, and giving her very essence in return. It was a beautiful thing, she mourned, which was hopelessly doomed. She had to protect herself now, or she would return to New York in worse shape than she had left it. She had thought Stu was right for her, and then suffered for her mistake. Now she knew Roberto was wrong for her; no amount of one-sided love could change that.

Wrapped in a cocoon of anguish, pure exhaustion—psychological and physical—finally claimed her. She fell into a state of willed unawareness, a deep stupor, a necessary escape into the depths of unconsciousness.

No sound disturbed her shallow peace. She remained immune to everything through the long night except her own need for survival. She was unaware of the low voices that trailed off only after several hours of camaraderie; she was unaware of others asleep in the clearing; she was unaware of the first light of dawn as it edged over the hilltops and glistened through the dew-gilded trees. It was only when a firm hand shook her shoulder—had she imagined a gentle touch to her cheek not a moment before?—that she reluctantly emerged from her protective shell to gather her things together and prepare to break camp.

Roberto had evidently excused her from breakfast chores, she surmised, as Paul approached her with a cup of steaming coffee and a plate of scrambled eggs. He studied her intently as he stood before her briefly. Eva avoided his eyes as she thanked him for the food and sat down to sip the coffee, wondering how much he suspected about her absence the night before. Two brothers, so alike yet so different. Paul could read her mind just as Roberto could, but while Paul used what he gleaned to understand and comfort her, Roberto used it to torment her.

"You okay?" he asked softly; then, at her affirmative nod, he turned back to the fire. She watched him go, then felt her gaze slip to Roberto who, having already finished his breakfast, was helping Carlos reload the donkeys' backs. He was so strong, so sure of himself, she had to admit; if only she could borrow some of that same strength and confidence, she would make it through this trip regardless of those deeper, more disturbing emotions.

The coffee had begun to really wake her up, and she was surprised at how well she felt. The evening's rest, as all-encompassing as it had been, had performed wonders on her body. Perhaps the open air—fresh and bracing—had aided the healing process. Whatever, concluded Eva with relief, she felt ready and able to face another day's hike, particularly knowing that she might see the Espinhaco Topaz before the day was out.

While the last of the cleaning up and packing was done, Eva took the opportunity to take more pictures. Her camera had been accepted as a bona fide member of the expedition by now, so she was able to photograph without drawing anyone's attention. As she snapped, she was also able to monitor the progress of the group through her lens so that she would in no way detain them when they were ready to move out. Thoroughly engrossed as she focused on Carlos untying the donkeys and leading them out of the clearing toward the path, she flinched at a curt order issued close to her ear.

"I can see where you get your practice. Now, if you can force yourself to stop caressing that fool black box, we can get going!"

Jolted by his sudden interruption of her concentration and embarrassed by the private meaning of his words, she reddened, grabbed her bags together indignantly, and strode away from Roberto with as much conviction as she could pretend to, knowing that he would be watching and enjoying her stormy exit.

The march resumed without further fuss, the pace a hearty one bolstered by the refreshing morning air. Eva had thrown her sweater over her shoulders against the early-morning chill, but the sun soon rose high enough to take its place on her bare arms. She enjoyed the hike today, her body having grown accustomed to both the packs and the steady pace, as she knew it would. The blisters on her heels were covered by the Band-Aids Roberto had given her, so she felt a minimum of discomfort from that quarter.

In fact, the only quarter from which she did feel discomfort was the emotional one. Having finally admitted to herself that she was in love with Roberto, she suffered the dull ache of desire at the thought of him. While her head told her one thing, her heart contradicted it. She was caught in the middle of an unabating battle between the forces of reason, which strove to eliminate Roberto from her mind, and the forces of passion, which could not function without his constant presence.

This inner war waged on as the small caravan covered ground, the undulating path challenging by its very vacillation. The terrain had grown more rugged by midmorning as the path showed signs of natural erosion. Eva kept up with the others easily, scrambling up the rocky rises, tumbling down the jagged declines, taking the occasional detour through the underbrush to skirt a blocked stretch of path.

Roberto, a distance from her at the head of the expedition, snapped out directives with an impatience that surprised her. She would have thought him to be in his glory with the arrival at the mine imminent. Something troubled him, making him uncharacteristically moody as they wound their way on. Eva assumed that the deterioration of the path worried him, and she wondered somewhat apprehensively what they would find at the end of their trek.

CHAPTER 6

The heat of the sun had begun to intensify once again, as the group paused to rest shortly after noon. The going had been more difficult than they had expected, so rather than plod through without stop to the mine, Roberto had readjusted their estimated arrival to the late afternoon. This, in addition to the taxing nature of the day's climb, warranted the midday rest.

Apprehension hung heavily among them as they rested and ate the small lunch that Jacques and Carlos had passed out. Roberto seated himself at a distance from Eva, she noted with a mixed sense of relief, and studied the map of the mine as he ate. She was sure that he already knew it by heart but was probably anticipating where the poorer conditions would be found, if his occasional brooding look was any indication of his thoughts.

Lunch behind them, they moved on. It was even warmer than it had been yesterday, and Eva sweated along with the rest of them. She was grateful for the cool tank top she had put on in the privacy of her bed-roll that morning, having all too clearly remembered the previous day's heat. She was also grateful for her natural curls, which in earlier years she had gone to such pains to straighten, but which now formed vibrant tendrils around her face, becoming her increasingly as the heat took its toll on all else. As they walked on, she cooled herself by securing the bulk of the hair in a casual topknot, leaving only loose wisps to mingle with the drops of perspiration at the sides of her face and on her neck. She was rather pleased with herself for managing both of her packs so well, although she did permit Tom to spell her occasionally with one of them.

As the afternoon wore on, the group moved more slowly, hampered both by the unpredictable terrain and by growing fatigue. By the time the sun had settled in its late-afternoon perch, casting long shadows through the tree branches, they heard a new sound piercing the silence of the mountainside. Water, somewhere just ahead—and they knew that they had reached their destination. Sure enough, several twists and turns around the hillside brought them to a waterfall, tumbling gently but gleefully across their path. No one complained as they passed beneath its cooling spray to negotiate one last turn. Only then did they emerge into a large clearing, dominated by the deserted mine entrance they had been seeking.

Shouts rang out from the front runners and Eva bounded forward to join in the spontaneous celebration, for not only had they reached the mine but its entrance stood clear and open, a welcome invitation for their exploration.

Roberto was the only one among them to remain detached from the broad grins and backslapping that took place. Even the ominous Pierre begrudgingly smiled his pleasure at their arrival at the mine, drawing Eva within the range of his enjoyment for the first time. Roberto, however, stood back, his hands on his hips and legs apart, studying the hillside out of which the mine had been carved. The soil was dry and of the red hue Eva had become so accustomed to, having to continually dust it off her sneakers, pants, and bags. As he regarded it now, his eye moved from the gaping entrance to the mound of earth that served as its roof, to the adjacent incline rising above it. He remained deeply engrossed in his examination as he moved from one side to another, scrutinizing every angle above, to the side of, and behind the mine entrance.

Eva took the opportunity of the otherwise light moment to use her camera. The sense of achievement, as premature as it really was, was so visible on the faces of these men she was coming to know so well that she couldn't resist photographing them. Changing the lens to a telephoto, she stood back and framed Tom's tongue-in-cheek exploration of the sides of the mine door, Jacques's own attempts at photographing the scene with his miniature camera, Pierre's victory pipe, its cherry-rich aroma wafting deliciously through the otherwise pure air, Paul's warm expression as he approached Roberto.

On this last frame she lingered long after she had made the exposure to study the two brothers. Although she was out of earshot, Paul's gestures seemed aimed at easing Roberto's tension, albeit without success. Eventually the two did find something to share a smile about; Eva suspected that it had little to do with the mine.

Camp was quickly made, the donkeys quartered by a clump of dwarf trees, the packs unloaded, and all muscles flexed into a sort of forced relaxation. Excitement ran high, though no one dared pose the one question everyone wanted to know the answer to. Finally, Jacques spoke up, the suspense too much.

"When do we go in, Roberto?" he asked, his lilting accent disguising any impatience he might have felt.

Roberto did not respond immediately, a look of mild concern on his face as he continued to analyze the terrain surrounding the mine. When he eventually spoke it was in a slow and hesitant voice, as though he was not quite sure of the answer himself.

"I think we'll try a preliminary exploration now, while there's still a little light. That hillside worries me. Do you see those indentations on the area behind the mine entrance?" he asked, the question purely rhetorical as he continued immediately. "It looks like the ground has sagged in some spots. There is also some erosion of the hill up here." He pointed to the wall of the mountain to the left that overlooked the mine's entrance. "I think we may have some work inside. Let's take a look."

He sorted through the supplies which were now on the ground and unrolled one of the canvas packages to remove some long search-type flashlights. Taking one himself, he tossed others to Paul and Pierre, who were standing closest to him. He motioned to Tom to grab the coils of heavy rope that lay on the ground near the flashlights, and then headed for the mine. Carlos was content to occupy himself with the remaining unpacking and perhaps a little nap, but the others moved forward to follow Roberto. Eva was as eager as the rest to see what they faced, but as they neared the entrance Roberto turned brusquely.

"You wait here, Eva, until we know something more. It could be difficult in the darkness inside."

"Oh, no!" she exclaimed, oblivious to the others looking on as she argued with Roberto. "I've got to go in. I'd really like to photograph what's there as you find it!" She was already fumbling in her camera bag to get the flash which she knew she would need in the black corridors of the mine.

"I don't want you coming in with us now, Eva," he repeated in a tautly held voice, his eyes boring into hers.

"Come on . . . I've come all this way and kept up with the rest of you. I've earned my right to go in now!" It was her best argument, but she knew from his expression that it was not good enough for him.

"You stay!" he growled, the fierceness of his tone raising several heads, then his voice softened to add, "If it's safe, you can go in to photograph later," and with that, he turned on his heel and led the men through the entrance, precluding any further discussion. Only Paul turned to look back at Eva, with a shrug of his shoulder and a sympathetic look, then she was left to smolder with no one for company but Carlos and his donkeys.

Like a dog, she fumed silently—he had ordered her to "stay" just like a dog. But what really upset her was not his order but the fact that she had obeyed him. It wouldn't have bothered her if she felt that he was really concerned with her safety; if that had been the case, she would have been flattered. But she was convinced that his refusal was one more attempt to humiliate her. He hadn't wanted her along on this trip to begin with, and now that she was he would make her regret it. How could she have fallen in love with a man who could be so cruel? The question tormented her and she had no solution for it.

Looking for a diversion to relieve her disappointment at not being allowed inside the mine, Eva remembered the waterfall around the turn, and gathering a few things together, she headed for it. The water, as it cascaded from the cliffs higher up, was cool and clear, a refreshing shower which Eva relished, having begun to feel grimy under the fine film of sweat and red dust that coated her skin. She splashed the water on herself, using the small bar of soap she had brought in her bag to cleanse her arms and face. The cool of the waterfall invigorated her, and in her condition of frustration, the temptation was too great. Within minutes she had stripped off her T-shirt and bra, wishing, though not quite daring, to go further, even knowing that the men were otherwise occupied. Bending at the waist, she soaped her hair under the renewing flow, allowing wayward sprinkles of the rinse to liberally moisten her body. Straightening again, she let water drip to the towel wrapped at her waistband. Falling from her saturated ringlets, it rippled down her neck and shoulders to trickle onto her breasts and back. As she reluctantly toweled herself dry, her terry-draped hand circled the fullness of her breast, bringing a sharp reminder of Roberto's caress which had electrified her so. Even as she recalled it, the rosy peaks grew to pebble-hardness, until she quickly drew on her clothes and broke the spell.

As she surmised, the men were still within the mine when she returned. She took the opportunity to apply some lipstick and blush-on, before she chose a spot in the fast-sinking sun to dry her hair. She was well into this undertaking, with most of the dampness evaporated from her now sparkling hair, when a low hum of voices signaled the men's return. Anxious to know what they had found, she jumped up to meet them, only to be halted, midway, by the unanimously grim faces that re-emerged into the sunlight, eyes squinting in reaction to the brightness which suddenly assaulted them.

"Bad news?" she asked fearfully, aiming the question at no one in particular. Roberto glared at her, a look of impatience in his eyes as he abruptly walked off in the direction of Carlos. Bewildered, she looked from one to the other of the remaining faces. It was Paul who took her elbow and led her apart from the others to explain.

"The shafts look pretty clear but a bit shaky, for two-thirds of the way down. The ropes barely held in some places. The main problem is what looks to be a collapse in the main shaft leading to the Topaz. We'll have to go in tomorrow with shovels, but Roberto is worried that the added equipment, not to mention the digging action, may trigger a further collapse. We're going to try to bolster up some of the weaker points before we dig. It's pretty discouraging!"

Paul's voice had been low; the others needed no further reminder of the situation. Eva listened without interruption, a sinking feeling overtaking her, too, by the time he had finished. Inexplicably, her first concern was for Roberto rather than for the danger itself.

"Roberto knew we could find almost anything," she began. "Was it that much of a shock? He looks furious," she added softly, casting a glance in his direction.

"No, it's not the Topaz that's his main worry. You're right; he knew the possibility of finding a collapse. That doesn't concern him as much as the danger involved in the digging. He feels a responsibility for all of us. He would be devastated if anyone was hurt in the process. You have to understand him, Eva. He's really a very moral person."

Eva wondered if there was a message between the lines for her. His last comment seemed to apply to more general things than the mine. He studied her expectantly now, awaiting a reply.

"Is he?" she asked, trying to prevent a deeper feeling from showing.

"You know he is," Paul stated factually, refusing to let the matter drop, challenging her to say more.

Eva was beginning to feel uncomfortable under Paul's penetrating gaze. She was sure he saw through her feeble attempts at feigning indifference. "How would I know? Roberto storms off in anger every time I get close to him!"

"I don't think you'd be attracted to an immoral person." Paul's innocent smile belied his not-so-innocent words.

Defensively, Eva flung back, "And just what makes you think I'm attracted to him?"

Now Paul's smile became one of gentle understanding, melting Eva's anger almost before his words were out. "I can see it in your eyes, Eva. It's written all over your face. Every time you look at him I see it. It's been there since that first night we all met. Even when he's putting you down, I see it. Are you in love with him?"

Silence hung between them as Eva pondered his question. Oh, she knew the answer well enough. But to acknowledge it? How had Paul known so positively? The knot inside her was so taut she knew she had no choice.

"Was it that obvious?" she asked sadly.

"Only to me, Eva. I know Roberto and now I've gotten to know you," he explained in his soft and sympathetic voice. "I can see the chemistry between you."

"It's funny," she looked at the ground, only occasionally daring to raise her eyes to him. "I left New York to get away from the pressures. I wonder if it's worse for me here."

"No, Eva. Love can never be worse. You know that! At any rate, with a little luck you'll have the Espinhaco Topaz to photograph. You'll really love that!"

She saw that he was purposely changing the subject and she wouldn't fight him. "Now you're comparing apples and oranges, Paul," she joked as she took a deep breath to signal the end of the subject. "So what's the plan for tomorrow?"

"We'll wait until everyone is rested and we have the

benefit of daylight, and we'll begin digging," he explained, seemingly as relieved as she to return to solid ground.

"What good will daylight do in the dark of the shafts?" Eva thought aloud, trying to follow his logic.

"Good question!" He smiled affectionately at her. "I asked Roberto the same question while we were still down there. It could clue us in on a particularly weak section in the upper level of the mine. In other words, if we see daylight we know we've got holes . . . and trouble!"

Aware of the situation, Eva now shared the concern of the others. "I'm sorry, Paul. What will I be able to do?" She doubted that Roberto would let her get near the mine, let alone in it, lest she be in the way during the sensitive digging.

Paul would not presume to second-guess Roberto, so he responded lightly, "Right now, you can give me a hand with supper!" They silently walked together to the food supplies, where they set to work.

That evening the atmosphere within the group was one more of psychological fatigue than physical. Concern was evident on all faces, although there was enough excitement in anticipation to make the evening a pleasant one. Even Roberto's humor improved as the evening wore on.

Eva excused herself early, suspecting that the men would be less inhibited if she were not there, and she wanted some time to herself anyway. She headed in the direction of the waterfall that had given her so much pleasure earlier that evening. The moonlight had filtered through the foliage enough to sprinkle silver dust liberally over the cascading water.

Sitting down on a large rock out of range of the droplets, she concentrated on the hypnotic rhythm of the falls as her mind retraced her earlier conversation with Paul. He had read her like a book, she mused. She had once told Roberto that Paul could be a best friend. Her instincts guided her well; she had confided in Paul as she would have confided in a best friend. Somehow she knew she could trust him to keep her secret. After all, he had betrayed nothing of Roberto's feelings, if indeed he knew them.

What saddened Eva more than what Paul had said was what he had not said. When she had admitted her love for Roberto, Paul had made no comment on it. She had a mental list of the things he could have said. He could have told her that she was much too vulnerable at this point to think herself in love; there was some truth to that. He could have told her that Roberto was all wrong for her; instead he had just acknowledged the chemistry at work between them. He could have made excuses for Roberto, saying that he was too busy to settle down or too concerned about the expedition to care for Eva or perhaps that he was involved with someone somewhere else; Paul had offered no such excuses. He could have said that Roberto liked her; but then, Paul would never have betrayed that information, even if it was true, which it wasn't. For although Eva knew that she could physically arouse Roberto, she also knew that she aggravated him more often than not.

What did she really know of Roberto? What did he do during the rest of the year? She knew he had taken over his father's business, but what exactly did he do? This puzzled Eva—she was in love with a man about whom she knew next to nothing. Her life had always been dominated by reason; now all of her theories about the mind ruling the body were being disproved. The feelings she had for Roberto had nothing to do with reason, yet she knew that they would be part of her forever.

Once again, as had happened the previous night, a

hand on her shoulder shattered her concentration, and she looked up half knowing that she would see Roberto standing above her. It was a repeat performance on a different stage, she thought, and she was still too raw from the last one to be able to handle another.

"I was just returning to camp," she lied, jumping to her feet and moving forward until Roberto barred her way, his strong body firmly planted before her. He had withdrawn his hand from her shoulder when she had risen, and now stood with his arms folded across his broad chest.

"Don't let me frighten you off. You had no intention of going back just yet. I just wanted to talk. I think I owe you an apology." The smile on his face, self-satisfied as it was at his own perceptiveness, fascinated her. And if he had an apology for her, she wanted to hear it.

"Go on," she ordered, keeping her voice stern.

"I shouldn't have spoken to you in front of the others the way I did this afternoon. It was wrong of me. I'm sorry." He seemed genuine enough, she thought.

But apology or not, her anger flared up at the reminder of the afternoon's humiliation. "You're damned right you owe me an apology! And I accept it. There was no reason why I couldn't have gone into the mine," she snapped.

His eyebrow arched at her response. "You misunderstand me. I would never have let you go into the mine this afternoon, and I was right about that, knowing what we now know about its safeness. I apologize for embarrassing you in front of the others."

"That figures," she countered sarcastically, then her eyes widened in alarm as she understood his further meaning. "You mean that you won't allow me to go in at all tomorrow? Roberto, you can't do that to me!" she pleaded.

"I certainly can, and I will." His dark eyes glared at her, daring her to argue. He was not disappointed.

"What gives you the right? I'm an adult. You don't have the authority to prevent me from doing what I want to do! Just who do you think you are?" She was approaching the boiling point, her hands on her slim hips, the flush of anger on her cheeks, her feet set in as firm a stance as his. She had no intention of budging.

Suddenly his face softened. A smile spread across his lips, his eyes narrowed with humor, sending laugh lines radiating from their corners to the crown of his cheekbones.

"You look terrific when you're angry! Maybe that's why I provoke you. It's so unusual to see a woman who stands up for things the way you do. You look very alive right now!"

"And you're trying to change the subject," she retorted, her anger abating somewhat under the warming glow of his expression.

"No, I won't do. that. And I won't let you go into the mine until I feel it is completely safe. I don't think I could live with myself if . . . it's my responsibility, don't you see?" Now he was the one who was pleading, or as close as a man such as he could come to it, she thought. His concern did touch her, though she warned herself that it meant absolutely nothing.

He put his hands gently on her shoulders, sending an involuntary thrill through her, as he reassured, "I know how much it means to you to go into the mine. If it is at all possible, you will. Trust me?"

Of course she would trust him, she knew. She would trust him to the ends of the Earth with her life, she was that far gone! How could she fight him? Regardless of his motivation, he was protecting her in a way that she craved.

His touch was already upsetting her balance, and

that she did have to fight. Gazing down at the hands on her shoulders with a look of alarm, she backed out of his grasp and added without looking up, "I have to get back now."

He spoke quickly, extending his hands out to the sides in a clear hands-off gesture. "No, please stay. Talk with me for a while. I promise I won't touch you, if that's what you want." His voice had lowered to a murmur at the last phrase, causing Eva to blush.

"Yes, that's what I want," she insisted, refusing his backhanded invitation before she could be further tempted. And a sweet temptation it was! Eva had always known of the strong passion within her, but this man had awakened it with a ferocity which frightened her, even as it excited her.

Roberto repeated his initial request, sensing that she would still bolt if he challenged her. "Come and sit. Tell me about your life in New York." He coaxed her softly, purposely seating himself first to let her choose her own distance. Eva could not turn down this more innocent invitation, as much as her better judgment told her to. She felt drawn too strongly to the man to deny herself the time with him, particularly given his gentlemanly assurance of pure conversation. She sat down a short distance from him, far enough to preclude physical contact yet close enough for easy conversation. She held herself stiffly, suddenly feeling awkward in the presence of this man whom she secretly loved. As always, he noticed her actions.

"Relax! I said I wouldn't touch you," he offered gently, his velvety command having its desired effect. "What kind of work were you involved in when you packed up to come down here?"

Eva did relax, especially when he broached such an interesting and indeed neutral subject. "I work for a newspaper group and had been given an assignment to photograph the old mansions in the area. Oh, I know it may sound dull to you," she went on quickly, "but it's exactly what I most love doing." Her eyes lit up in proof of her statement. "I love being in the houses, to begin with. They are so dignified, so rich in history, interesting in a way new houses never could be. You know, winding staircases, hidden niches." She blushed at her own excitement. "I guess I'm a romantic at heart," she added shyly.

"I know what you mean." *About the houses or me,* Eva wondered. "Wasn't it difficult to photograph the dark interiors?" he went on.

"That's where the real challenge came in. You have to use wide-angle lenses and lots of floodlights. I was even going to try some light painting for eerie effects when . . ." She paused but then realized she should finish what she'd begun, ". . . when Stu took sick."

"Was your marriage a happy one?" His forwardness took her by surprise.

"Isn't that overstepping your bounds?" she snapped, pulling herself together quickly.

He responded softly, his expression so sincere that Eva melted once again. "I'm just curious. I won't hold it against you!" he teased.

Once more helpless to deny his request, she raised sad eyes to his. Speaking almost inaudibly, she began. "No. My marriage was not a happy one. It was a terrible mistake. I was all wrong for Stu. I couldn't make him happy. We disagreed about nearly everything. I guess I jumped into marriage at a vulnerable time for me. My parents had recently died; I felt very alone. Stu wanted me then. After the first few months we had very little to say to one another in a civil tone." She lowered her eyes in shame. "But this is wrong of me to be saying. Stu is dead."

Roberto broke in forcefully, "No, Eva, it needs to be

said. You can't keep it bottled up inside, or it will explode at some point . . . maybe in the arms of a stranger." The last he added in a lower, more husky tone of an afternoon remembered.

Color flooded onto Eva's cheeks at the memory, though mercifully the moonlight hid the extent of her embarrassment. "I usually am able to control myself," she defended herself somewhat apologetically. "I'm afraid I made a fool of myself that day," she added, half to herself.

Roberto had been watching her intently. Now he looked off in the distance as he flexed his denim-clad legs into a more comfortable position. Even in the moonlight Eva could see the rich outline of his shoulders straining against the fabric of his shirt and the sturdiness of his neck. She thought him, in that moment in the dim light, with his black hair and dark features at peace, the most handsome figure she had ever seen.

"No, Eva, you didn't make a fool of yourself. You merely discovered that you have weaknesses like the rest of us!"

Now it was Eva's turn to joke, albeit with a twist of seriousness. "And what are your weaknesses, Roberto?"

"My weaknesses?" he began with pretended pensiveness. "My major weakness right now seems to be an attractive young widow who turns me on!" His voice had taken on the huskiness which Eva now recognized as his own desire.

Annoyed as she was by the implication of his remark, she felt too close to success at getting him to talk about himself to object to his undertone. Instead, she totally ignored it and went on. "What kind of work do you do, Roberto, when you're not off hiking through the mountains?"

He smiled slyly, a twinkle of moonlight catching in

his eye as he glanced at her. "Taking a different tack, are you? Okay, I said we'd play by your rules." He became more serious and hesitated, studying the cascading waterfall before answering in a steady, businesslike tone. "I own a coffee plantation just west of São Paulo. It's quite large and quite successful. It has led me into other business ventures. I've been fortunate." There was an odd sense of resignation as he revealed this seemingly harmless information, and he paused and looked straight at Eva, as though expecting to catch some immediate reaction to his words. When she had none, he seemed puzzled but continued on. "I spend most of the year in Brazil but I do make frequent trips to the States for business and to visit . . ."

"Your mother?" she interrupted.

"Yes," he replied with a tenderness of tone which touched Eva. "I don't get to see her as often as I'd like, but I try to whenever possible. She's alone now."

"You seem very fond of her," Eva probed, her innate curiosity getting the better of her.

"Of course I'm fond of her. She's my mother!" he snapped, his impatience at her pointed questions growing by the minute. "My mother is a fine person who had some rough breaks in life. I'm very close to her now . . . though I spent my earliest years resenting her." The last was said almost as an afterthought, tempering the anger which had crept into his voice. Bringing his thoughts back to the present, he continued, "In answer to your original question, I keep busy."

Whatever possessed Eva to confront him she would never know. "I suppose you have a girl in every port, as they say?"

"Are you jealous?" he countered, avoiding a direct answer. There remained a certain tension in his attitude which had not been there earlier.

—115—

"Jealous? Me, the widow? Of course not!" she snapped sarcastically. "I was just curious."

His taunting voice came at her again. "You have nothing to be jealous about, you know." Oh, she knew well enough! He despised her; she would never be in competition with his women. He might desire her, but only for the physical gratification. He would never love her as she loved him, she was sure.

Eva didn't respond to his taunt. What could she say? She felt within her the awful void she knew she was going to have to learn to live with. Unrequited love was something for soap operas; she would have to draw herself above it.

Trying to hide the despondency that had so quickly overtaken her, she rose from the rock on which she had been perched. In a voice echoing her sadness she explained, "I've got to go back now. Good night, Roberto."

He had jumped up within seconds of her doing so, and was now at her elbow, his hand stopping her exit. "Are you all right?" he asked, a tone in his voice that she didn't recognize.

"I just have to g-go, Roberto," she stammered, his closeness not only thwarting her plans for escape but also triggering the response within her which she feared most.

"I want you, Eva. You must know that," he crooned softly, taking her chin in his fingers and turning her face to his. Tears had begun to gather behind her eyelids, and he must have felt the tremble of her chin.

He tilted her head toward his, raising his other hand to frame her jaw, as his lips slowly descended to meet hers. So light and feathery was his touch that Eva quivered even more at the sweet tenderness. She returned the caress of his kiss, her lips the only means she had of conveying the love welling inside her.

Oh, she wanted him, too. How badly, he would never know. But she would be hurt worse if she gave into his possession than she was bound to be anyway. It took every fiber of her strength to pull back from his inviting embrace, but in diverting her strength such, she lost control of the tears that lined her lids. As they began to course down her cheeks, she begged him, "Please, Roberto. I can't . . ." Torture was written in the gaze she turned up at him as she sobbed, "Please . . ."

The coldness in the eyes, moments before brimming with passion and tenderness, bit into her, increasing her suffering tenfold. When he abruptly released her, she turned blindly and stumbled back toward camp, her vision blurred by the tears of pain that raged unchecked.

CHAPTER 7

Sleep was a long time coming for Eva that night. She felt exhausted, both physically and mentally. The hiking had been strenuous, the night air of the mountain enervating. But she lay awake until long after everyone else in the camp had succumbed to the much-needed rest.

Torment was eating her from the inside out. Her love for Roberto, his hatred of her, her guilt over Stuart, her failure as a wife—the tug-of-war continued endlessly. Given the opportunity, Eva would have immediately left Brazil. It was Roberto's nearness which punished her most. She was trapped, unable to return even to Terra Vermelho without a guide. And each time she saw him glaring at her, she felt the knife twist a little more in her gut. When she finally did doze, it was into a fitful sleep which merely transferred the anguish into a dream setting. It didn't surprise her when Roberto stopped beside her before breakfast.

"You look terrible. Didn't you sleep?" he mocked her, a satanic look in his eyes which promptly unbalanced her already tentative composure.

"That's really none of your business!" she snapped back softly, so that none of the others would see her oversensitivity and jump to a conclusion as to its cause. She didn't relish another public argument, despite any apology.

"It certainly is my business when I'm trying to keep this expedition going," he retorted, his voice held low for similar reasons.

"Don't worry. I'm in very good health. You won't be stuck with a malaria victim, I can guarantee!" she spoke sarcastically, then stalked away from him toward the fire and a cup of morning coffee, which she badly needed.

Roberto and the five other men—even Carlos had been drafted, to his obvious chagrin, to help with the digging—loaded themselves up with equipment and entered the mine shortly after breakfast. Eva was in no mood for arguments, particularly ones which she knew she'd lose, so she didn't push Roberto to let her join them. It did seem easier to trust him for the time being, as much as it galled her to do so. After all, he had assured her that she would be able to go in as soon as it was safe enough.

Not wanting to appear to be sulking, she had helped the men don their backpacks and balance their gear, though she made a point of avoiding Roberto. If he was so damned sure of himself, he could just do his own packing, she fumed inwardly.

Once the group had been swallowed up by the long, dark corridors of the mine, Eva turned back to the camp to clean up from breakfast. She spent the morning impatiently trying to find things to do. She picked up this, neatened up that, moved the other thing. She even did some photographing, but what was usually such a diversion for her was now no help in easing her frustration.

Pacing around the camp like a caged animal, she found herself stopping beside Roberto's things. Impulsively she sat down and let her hand trace the curved outline of the rolled sleeping bag he had so recently slept in. Using it as a pillow, she lay down in the sunlight to let its warming rays soothe her. To her begrudging pleasure, however, the real soothing effect came from the pillow that now cushioned her red-highlighted curls. The faintest traces of that fresh and masculine smell she associated with Roberto reached her nostrils, calming her, entrancing her into a peaceful, albeit brief, nap.

The nearness of him, if by smell alone, had given her comfort, and when she awoke, perhaps an hour later, she felt greatly improved from earlier in the morning. With a fresh cup of coffee in her hand, she explored the outer perimeters of the camp, which she had never seen.

Refreshed as she was, she took more pictures, this time becoming engrossed in her subject matter. She photographed the landscape, dominated by its dual hues of the dull green of the foliage and the red of the mineral-rich soil. Adding a polarizing filter to her camera, she photographed the clouds which, more numerous today than on any other day she had been here, scampered across the purplish-blue sky in ever-changing conformations.

As she watched, the sun caught on something white off in the distance. To Eva's surprise and delight, it was the steeple of a church in a distant village, barely visible except when the sun singled it out from between the cloud shadows. Quickly, Eva put on the longest telephoto lens she had brought with her and raised the camera to her eye. She may have waited another ten or fifteen minutes thus, until the sun and the clouds had arranged just the right compromise. Only at that moment did she make the exposure, and she instantly knew that it was to be one of the better ones of the trip. It was all in the lighting, she thought with satisfaction, aware that her patience had paid off.

If only patience paid off in other realms! She had infinite patience when it came to photography. Why did she have so little patience when it came to Roberto, she demanded of herself angrily. Her show of temper only made him all the more stubborn. Maybe if she tried a different tactic, the remainder of this trip could be salvaged. Yes, that was what she would do, she resolved. She wouldn't challenge him head-on anymore— if she could help it. It was a big "if," she knew, but she had to convince herself that she could attain the same end by different, and hopefully more peaceful, means.

It was easier said than done. Eva's boredom had returned with a vengeance by the time the men finally emerged from the mine in the early afternoon. They all appeared exhausted, with dirt heavy in the folds of their clothes and smudged on their skins where it had mingled with sweat.

Eva knew enough to respect their somber expressions and save her questions until they had had a chance to rest. She helped wherever she could, getting out the lunch while they cleaned up at the waterfall, applying Band-Aids to open blisters, desperately working to curb her curiosity all the while.

It was Roberto who finally approached her when she had moved a distance from the others, and began to explain what had taken place.

"We were able to bolster some of the weaker places. Then we started digging out the collapse in the main shaft leading to the Topaz. It's going pretty well, but it's tiring. So far, the torches are holding up all right; if our hands and backs do, we may have a chance of breaking through later this afternoon." Throughout the delivery of this brief bulletin, his voice had been factual and devoid of emotion.

Eva made no answer. Impulsively she reached down for his right hand and lifted it to examine the welts on his fingers and palms. Stifling a wince, she looked him directly in the eye, playing his own game, she thought, and ordered, "Wait here!" while she ran to get the first-aid kit.

"You're a fine one to talk. You watch out for everyone else but ignore your own potential infections," she scolded, subconsciously adding the force of her own morning's frustration to her voice. She couldn't hide the anger as she went on, "You're so concerned about your responsibility for everyone else's safety. I suggest you watch out for yourself a little more!"

He had watched and listened with amusement as she had cleaned and covered the sores, overlooking her chiding tongue until her last statement. Suddenly he bristled.

"When I want your suggestions I'll ask for them," he growled; then, as suddenly, he was teasing again, adding in a low voice, "Aren't you making a big thing out of a few blisters? I think you enjoy holding my hand . . ."

Eva looked up to his face, her eyes conveying at his intimation the fury that words would have normally done. Abruptly she dropped his hand, slammed the first-aid kit onto the ground, and turned on her heel and walked away from him, her clenched fists the only remaining signs of her indignation.

She successfully avoided him until the group was ready to re-enter the mine. Since he seemed to have no intention of raising the issue himself, she knew it was up to her. Determined to test out her new tactic, she approached him quietly and asked calmly, "Can't

I go in this time, Roberto?" The only sign of pleading was in the green eyes that searched his for some warmth.

There was none. Coldly and dispassionately he replied, "Not now. You stay up here untill I tell you otherwise."

Eva opened her mouth to object, then closed it again in anticipation of the humiliation she would inevitably suffer if she argued with him. She just stood her ground and glared at him. To add to her fury, he sensed her thoughts and, adding salt to the wound, sent a twinkle of the eye and a smirk of the lips in her direction before entering the mine himself.

This wasn't working, fumed Eva, as the last of the men disappeared once again. *Nothing works with that man! He is a demon!* Her heart beating rapidly in agitation, she resumed her impatient vigil, all the while trying to decide what her next tactic should be.

She didn't quite know when the thought came to her, but she found herself calmly gathering her camera things together, reaching for one of the spare flashlights that lay with the other extra gear, and heading for the mine. She was an adult, she had told him, and as such she could chart her own course. Though she hadn't thought much about this one, common sense told her to follow the main shaft until her ears directed her otherwise. She was well guided, her torch lighting the way as she cautiously proceeded through the long corridor.

It seemed as though she had been walking for an hour when she finally stopped. As she moved forward she listened as carefully as she could; she heard nothing, no signs of digging or any other activity. The winding of the corridor itself had long since obliterated the light from the mine's entrance. Eva paused at each of the side shafts branching off the main one, but she had seen no indications of which one the men might have taken.

Reluctantly, she realized that she would do better to return to the camp until she could get some sort of guide better than mere hunch and hearing. She retraced her steps; *as always,* she mused, *the return trip appears shorter.* It was with relief that she caught the first rays of light filtering in through the mine entrance.

Her relief was short-lived. As she approached the opening, her camera equipment jangling gently against her hip, a shadow fell across her path, its source looming in the center of the doorway before her. She knew the profile on sight—the wide stance, the slim hips on which powerful hands rested, the firm torso, the broad shoulders, and the wide-brimmed hat hiding from her any view of his face. Even without seeing it, she suspected what that face held.

Not a word was spoken. Eva stopped short in front of him and peered into the shadowed countenance with as much determination as she could summon, given the verbal tirade she momentarily expected. She had passed to the side of him and emerged into daylight when the force broke loose. Wheeling around, he clamped a steel vise on her arm and half-dragged her from the entrance toward the opposite end of the camp, where he threw her roughly against the widest tree he could find, imprisoning her with arms on either side of her head, and glared at her. Eva noted that the camp was deserted except for him, mild solace given the circumstances.

"I told you to wait here!" he growled through his teeth. "Where were you? What were you doing in there?" If he had physically beaten her, she would have felt no more battered than she did now from the venom of hatred flowing at her. A worse punishment he could not have conceived.

"I was bored and just wanted to explore a little," she explained timidly, not wanting to confess that she had really wanted to find the digging but had failed.

"You were bored? I'm down there expecting cave-ins any minute and you're bored? Don't you know what can happen in there if you don't know what you're doing?" he snarled, forcefully, his upper lip curling to reveal the perfect whites beneath.

"I know what can happen, Roberto. Believe me, I just walked down the main shaft for a bit. That's all. I couldn't get lost. I was nowhere near the collapse you were working on." She spoke as calmly and quietly as she could, not wanting to make things worse with her own impetuosity.

His face was close to hers, his gaze locking it into immobility. The nearness, though at no points did their bodies touch, and the smell of him melted her anger and turned it to sadness. *How much he despises me,* she pondered; *if only that same force was love, it might come close to matching mine in intensity.*

"I just don't believe how stupid you can be, Eva!" the steely voice continued. "Where is your common sense!" he yelled, grabbing her shoulders and shaking her violently back and forth until her head reeled.

Weakly she whispered, "Don't, Roberto. You're hurting me!" and he promptly released her shoulders and let her slide down the bark of the tree to the ground, her knees too fluid to support herself. She let her head fall forward onto her bent knees, as she fought desperately to dispel the feeling of nausea that lurked in her middle.

"I should beat the living daylights out of you, you little bitch!" he seethed almost inaudibly, his venom once again lashing into Eva, who remained with her head down, unable to face his hostility. But Roberto had not yet finished.

"So help me, Eva, if you try that again I'll send you back to Terra Vermelho with Carlos. He's great at taking care of stubborn mules!" he raged at her, before stalking off to pick up several additional picks and then re-enter the mine.

When everything was quiet and Eva knew he had gone, she yielded to the few low sobs that had gathered in her throat during his onslaught. She didn't know how long she sat there, but finally she regained enough strength to get up and place her camera gear in the duffel. She knew of only one spot that would soothe her, and after gathering together a towel, soap, and clean clothes, she headed for it.

In sharp distinction from the thunder clouds that seemed to envelop her, the waterfall was playing gleefully over the rocks, sparkles of sunlight joining the merry game. Eva could not resist the infectiousness of its laughter for long, and her cloud gradually dispersed as she trailed her fingers through the ripples. Of all the sights she had seen so far on this trip, it was this spot that enchanted her the most. It was so clean and pure and simple—a garden of Eden, she mused, with temptations all around but only beauty at its core.

The music of the water cascading onto the rocks came as a lullaby, easing her tension and sending her into a kind of hypnotic state of relaxation. Without a second's hesitation, she drew off all of her clothes and submitted her naked body to the therapeutic pulsation of the waterfall. How good it felt to lean back against the cool, wet rocks and become part of the scenery in this second Eden. She shampooed her hair and soaped herself, letting the massaging rhythm of the falls remove the suds one by one and send them shimmering down her body to her toes, thence on to play hide-and-seek among the rocks below. She cleared her mind of everything except the regenerating effect of the water. It was only after a long time, when she had begun to shiver from its cool temperature, that she reluctantly pulled herself out of the water's range. An aura of peacefulness protected her. She dried herself and pulled on her panties and jeans, then choose a large, flat rock in the sun to bask on. Although the air was typically warm for the midafternoon, she had done nothing today to overheat herself, and the coolness of the water had indeed chilled her. Thus her every pore drank in the sunlight, its warmth drying the water droplets that lingered on her shoulders and breasts.

Closing her eyes, she sighed with pleasure as the gentle rays cast their halo of warmth over her. *This is my own garden of Eden,* she reflected, a smile breaking through the even glow of the sun on her face. *I could stay like this forever,* she declared silently.

She must have dozed off, lying as she was on the rock, when a distant noise broke through the haze of consciousness. Opening her eyes, she saw that the sun had disappeared behind billowing clouds, taking its protective robe from her. She sat up to go for her clothes when her eye froze on Roberto's tall, lean form lounging casually against a tree, his gaze glued to her.

Instinctively, she lifted her arms to cover her bare breasts, a combination of anger and embarrassment bringing a flush to her cheeks. "What are you, some kind of peeping Tom?" she snapped.

"Don't cover yourself. You really are beautiful," his velvety voice commanded through a broad smile as his eyes dropped to her breasts, caressing them until Eva felt them firm under her own protective hands.

"May I have my clothes, please?" He stood right next to them and she didn't quite trust herself to approach him, the tremors of arousal involuntarily beginning.

"No. You'll have to come and get them."

"Please throw them to me, Roberto."

"Come and get them. I have something to show you anyway, when you're ready to come over here." His teasing tone and mischievous grin hinted at some other source of excitement than the one Eva was already acutely aware of. She sensed that there had to be some explanation for his sudden turnaround in mood.

As though to underscore his words, Roberto stooped and picked up her bra and T-shirt and tucked them under his arm with an even more devilish twist of his lips.

"What is it?" Suddenly it dawned on her. "The Topaz! Roberto, did you reach the Topaz?" she shrieked, momentarily forgetting her immediate predicament. At his confirming nod and continuing grin, Eva jumped up and ran to him, her hands still crisscrossed on her chest.

"Let me see! Come on!" she bubbled with an enthusiasm as much due to the lightness of his mood as to the discovery of the gem.

Slowly he pulled a small, pink-yellow piece of stone from his pocket. It was breathtaking, even without the sun's electrification. As she stood mesmerized by its raw beauty, he explained.

"This is only a small crystal which we found nearby. The Topaz itself is on a higher ledge. We need different equipment to remove it, now that we've broken through. We'll be able to get it out tomorrow morning. I left the others finishing the digging down there so it should be safe."

Eva hadn't taken her eyes from the topaz. "It's beautiful, Roberto. I can't begin to picture an even larger piece of that magnificence!" Slowly she raised her eyes to his. "Thank you for coming out to show me. I appreciate it!" *Could he see how much,* she wondered.

His smile became mischievous again as he replaced

the crystal into his pocket. "There's a price, Eva." Without another word, he placed his hands onto her wrists and, despite the resistance of her arms against his, he slowly and steadily drew them away from her chest, laying open to his gaze the graceful curves of her full breasts, their rosy centers firmed in excitement. Her eyes never left his as they took in this, her own raw beauty.

When she could bear his gaze no longer, she lowered her head and begged him, "Roberto, please don't."

His forefinger cupped her chin and drew it up, and he looked into her eyes as he spoke softly, gently, "You're beautiful, Eva. You're a gem in your own right."

His words and their underlying sensuality captivated her. She was helpless to resist when he lowered his lips to reverently kiss the breasts that lay bare to his touch. Her nerve ends came alive, each one tingling with the passion that had begun to build within her. A moan of ecstasy slipped through her lips as his continued their exploration over her soft, ivory flesh, his tongue further tantalizing the buds which had swelled to their fullest.

Eva had to reach to his shoulders for support, her knees weakened by the quivering of her limbs. She buried her face in his dark hair, stroking it, kissing it, until she felt herself drawn down to her knees, then eased onto her back by Roberto's powerful grasp. She was totally under his spell now. Her heart thudded noisily within her as she watched him remove his shirt. His need matched hers, she knew; it was the one thing they shared.

Eva grasped in pure delirium as he lowered his warm body over hers, her breasts against his hair-roughened chest. It was flesh against flesh, man against woman in the most basic interchange of life. She writhed beneath him in eagerness to touch every inch of his skin.

In one tender moment Roberto raised his mouth from hers to gaze into her eyes. He spoke in the low and husky tone that excited her all the more.

"You were well named, Eva. You are an Eve in this garden of Eden. You belong here, lying naked on that rock. The only difference is that . . . you are wearing blue jeans," he murmured, his eyes twinkling suggestively as his hand seared a path down her abdomen onto her thigh and then back again, sending currents of desire through her.

She could only manage a breathless "Roberto" before his lips possessed hers with the urgency of exploding passion. She clung to him weakly, his hardness so electrifying to her, and returned his caresses with such ardor that neither of them noticed that it had begun to rain until the drops fell steadily from his shoulders onto hers.

"Roberto! It's raining!" Eva managed to cry out between kisses. She was only well aware of his fear of a heavy rainstorm and what it could do to the mine.

"Oh, my God, the mine! I've got to get the men out of the mine!" he bellowed, jumping up, grabbing for his shirt, and putting it on as he ran in the direction of the mine without a glance back at Eva.

She lay stunned where he had left her, ravished by the depths of passion which had been aroused and then abruptly abandoned. It was only when the rain began to fall heavily that she dressed and returned to the camp to await the men.

Trying to anticipate what would need to be done, Eva moved whatever she could under cover. The rain had reached torrential strength by the time the men finally emerged from the mine.

As had been the case earlier, they were weary and dirty, the latter problem being remedied by the rain, falling fast and steady. Roberto and Paul erected a makeshift tent to stow as much gear as possible out of the rain; the rest was put under the protective shelter of an overhang well in front of the mine entrance. It was under this overhang that, though soaked to the skin already, they took shelter to wait out the storm.

With all of the frantic activity, Eva had not been able to dwell on the scene that the rain had interrupted. Now, as the idle waiting began, she wrapped her arms around herself in sudden remembrance. How beautiful Roberto had been, so tender and giving. She could have almost imagined that he did love her, so gentle was his lovemaking, although she knew to the contrary. The thought of all that passion lost brought a look of deep sadness to her eyes.

"Are you cold?" Roberto's cool voice broke into her reverie, his eyes pointing out her wrapped arms as explanation for his inquiry.

Eva looked quickly up at him, then down again to the ground, needing time to erase the pain she knew he would see in her eyes. "Ah . . . no!" She realized she had to think of something to say to change the subject. "Do you think this rain will last long?" she asked, finally able to raise her head. He searched her face with unfathomable eyes before he ventured an answer.

"It shouldn't last too long. Torrential downpours don't usually last too long, but you never can tell." He peered out at the rain with concern on his face. "I only hope our work hasn't upset things . . ."

"What do you mean? Your digging certainly had nothing to do with the rain!" she countered, tongue-in-cheek.

He found no humor in her answer. "Of course not! But the danger with rains such as this is a cave-in. Often, over time, the mine shaft collapses at a weak point and the collapsed area itself strengthens the rest of the shaft, leaving one solid section. When we dug a passage to get to the Topaz, we broke through that one solid section; that entire area of the mine may be weakened as a result," he explained with obvious annoyance, both at the situation and at Eva.

Tom, who had been standing nearby, broke in, "So there's absolutely nothing we can do? We just stand here and watch it collapse?"

Roberto answered him with more control in his voice, Eva noted, than he had shown to her. "It may not collapse. We can't be sure. But, no, there's absolutely nothing we can do in either case. We can't go into the mine now and risk being caught. We can only hope this damned rain will stop soon!" he grunted, looking toward the sky, which was as ominous as ever.

He seemed to be struggling with himself for not having been better prepared for this occurrence. Voicing his rationale, he explained, "During these summer months it doesn't rain very often, but when it comes, it really comes! In torrents, as you can see! Actually, there's nothing we would have been able to do to better deal with the rain. It's just that we've come so close . . ." He shook his head with worry, having verbalized the unanimous sentiment of the group.

There was nothing to do but wait. Eva stared out at the rain from beneath the overhang. The torrents had created a waterfall . . . much like Eva's own. For that was exactly how she thought of it—as her own waterfall. Ironic that Roberto had said it too: Eve, in the garden of Eden. The temptation was so great there. She wasn't sure she would have been able to deny Roberto had not the rain begun. The strength of her own desire frightened her almost as much as her loss of conscience in his arms. Yes, she would have indeed bitten from the apple, she feared, but for this other act of nature.

She felt his eyes on her even before she looked up to find Roberto gazing at her. Their lines of vision locked and held, cemented together by some unknown fiber. It was only a low and ominous rumbling, steadily growing louder and louder, which broke the spell.

CHAPTER 8

Eva saw the alarm in Roberto's eyes even before he raised them to the overhang as it began to crumble.

"Landslide! Get away from here!" he yelled, alerting the others and grabbing Eva's hand as he pushed any lingering bodies out from under the overhang. They ran to the opposite side of the camp, horrified, watching the entire overhang as it collapsed into thousands of fragments of wet earth, rock, and grass, a thunderous hail of debris, completely obliterating the protective niche where they had stood short moments before. Mud continued to slide from the hillside high above the plateau on which they had camped, accumulating in huge, water-soaked mounds on top of the gear they had stowed beneath the overhang's deceitful safety.

The noise was deafening—a cacophony of rain hitting mud, mud hitting stones, stones hitting stones as they fell. The braying of the donkeys joined the clamor as Carlos and Pierre led them to a safer place further from the hillside.

Having deposited Eva with a shove at the side of the camp farthest from the danger, Roberto yelled orders above the din to the others, who joined him in the frantic removal to that side of anything that had not yet been buried in the mud slide. They then could do nothing but stand by with Eva, eyes wide in dread at what was taking place before them.

Suddenly, Tom bolted from the relative safety of their present vantage point and headed for the mine, shouting over his shoulder, "The shovels! A couple of them are just inside the entrance to the mine! We'll need them if . . ." His voice was lost in the roar of the rain as it pelted more violently than ever on the mud-caked earth.

He was too close to the mine entrance to see the tremor of the earth above the mine when it began. Rippling its way down the hillside, from within as well as without, the flooded earth broke loose from its moorings and crashed onto the roof of the mine, demolishing it with one giant explosion of soil, rocks, and timber fragments.

Roberto barged forward, Paul close behind, just as the final collapse took place. Eva gasped in horror, her eyes witnessing a tangling of arms and legs and mud and stone. The domino action inevitably followed, each of the ribboning indentations, which Roberto had eyed so dubiously the day before, caving in, to be filled by a mélange of displaced earth and uprooted foliage, even as Roberto and Paul managed to pull Tom free of the ongoing havoc.

The moment of panic seemed infinite, frozen in Eva's view until she saw Tom weakly struggle to his feet under his own power. She dashed forward to assist, but he was well escorted by Paul and Roberto through the torrents to their observation station.

Knowing that Tom was all right, the group turned and watched the last of the ruin as it played itself out before their eyes. What had been a mine door, clear and open when they had first arrived yesterday, was now nothing more than a sodden hill under which was buried hours of labor, much of their gear, all of their hopes . . . and the Espinhaco Topaz.

The storm continued at full strength for no more than a few minutes before it tapered off to a drizzle and then was done. As Eva shared the vigil with the others, no words were spoken. With the last of the raindrops came an excruciating silence, settling oppressively over the dismal scene. There was nothing to say. The voice of nature had said it all.

It was almost, reflected Eva, as though some greater force had determined that the Topaz should remain out of the reach of man for another hundred and fifty years. The brunt of the destruction had seemingly been aimed at the mine; once it was sealed, locked away from man's touch, the torrents had ended. Nature's fury had been spent.

As the shock of defeat held them immobile, the clouds slowly dissipated and the sun appeared once again, low in the late-afternoon sky, dancing on the raindrops that lingered on rocks, glistening on the moisture that clung to the foliage, reflecting in the mirrorlike puddles that were virtually everywhere. The sun's very cheerfulness at having returned to sparkle on the hillside did nothing to ease the depression which the weary adventurers felt.

Roberto took charge, as always. "Let's get this mess cleaned up and see where we stand," he ordered, his tone just barely conveying the disappointment his face so openly wore.

Eva pitched in with the others, as they unearthed from the top layer of saturated earth the few things that had survived the worst of the landslide. Most of these things either had been destroyed outwardly by the force of the rocks or were so deeply infused with mud and grit that they were beyond use. Several of the knapsacks were among the latter, their contents unusable until they could be properly sorted out and washed.

Most of the food supply was intact, to everyone's relief. Not that there was an ounce of appetite among them now, but it was obvious to all that they would need food for the return trip to Terra Vermelho. With the exception of some hopelessly water-logged bread, this would not be a problem.

The warming rays of the sun began to dry Eva's wet clothes, although the rummaging through the muck had left a muddy boot from her knees down. The men were in even worse shape, spattered from head to foot, the iron-red hue of the marshy mounds giving the impression of smeared blood. *The blood of the earth,* Eva bemoaned, as she stood back to watch the last of the salvageable gear being extracted from the still oozing soil.

The analogy had been too vivid for Eva's churning stomach. Aware of a sharp wave of nausea, she turned away from the men and escaped to a wet, though clean, rock onto which she sank. Fortunately, several deep breaths controlled the spasm, but she remained as she was, her head lowered on her hands, which in turn rested on her bent knees.

Then a strong hand was on her neck, massaging it briskly to get the blood circulating again, and Roberto's soothing voice commanded her, as it had done so often, to relax.

Eva hadn't realized how strongly the trembling was shaking her body until the steadiness of his grasp exaggerated it by comparison. She remained where she was, taking deep breaths, until she felt strong enough to raise her head.

"I'm all right now. Thanks," she offered in a weak voice without looking at Roberto.

"Are you sure? This has been pretty harrowing." His concern touched her, although she knew he considered it his duty as the leader of the expedition to look out for the health, mental and physical, of its members.

She nodded in his direction. "Yes. I'm sure. It just hit me all of a sudden. Those mud spatters look so like blood . . ." Her voice trailed off as she realized that it had been the sight of this bloody hue on Roberto which had disturbed her most. How close they had all come to being crushed in the landslide! But if anything had happened to Roberto, she would have been doubly crushed.

Now Roberto took her arm, gently but firmly, and led her out of her corner in the direction she knew so well, toward the waterfall. She turnd questioning eyes on him, but he had anticipated her reaction and already had a finger before his lips in a sign for her to keep still. In a loud voice he addressed the others, each of whom looked more bedraggled than the next.

"I suggest that we all wash this grit off before we lose the sun entirely. We look like we've been through a bloody battle and I'm afraid it's making Mrs. Jordenson sick!" He winked at her, a twinkle in his eye, as he proceeded to guide her to the falls.

She looked at him with astonishment. "How can you make jokes after what just happened?" Incredulity had raised her voice several notes.

He shrugged his shoulders in resignation as he bent to bathe his arms in the rushing flow of the water. "What would you have me do, Eva? I'm as disappointed —no, more so—than the rest of you. I've been looking forward to bringing out the Topaz for a long time." He paused, a faraway look in his eyes. His voice carried some of his regret when he continued. "I'm glad my old friend from Terra Vermelho didn't live to see this, after seeing the map pass through his family for years." He looked up, reminded once again of Eva's presence. "At least no one was hurt. It's done, Eva. We tried. Who could ask more?"

With that, he finished his clean-up and headed back to camp. Eva quickly washed her own arms and hands, then dunked her legs, sneakers and all, in the water, convinced that she'd rather be soaked anew than branded by the treacherous earth-turned-fluid for a few such destructive moments.

Reluctant to return to the scene of the devastation just yet, she was relieved when Jacques appeared to wash at the falls.

"Do you mind if I dry off here in the sun while you wash?" she asked, mindful of his possible desire for privacy.

"*Mais non,* Eva! By all means, stay where you are. I'd like the company." His friendliness warmed her inside as the sun began its work outside.

"Tell me, Jacques. Roberto seems to have recovered. Now you seem in good spirits, too. Aren't you terribly disappointed?" she asked, returning his friendly tone.

"Of course I am! But, you see, I am a businessman, like Roberto. And a successful one, if I may add." His smile was so sincere that she couldn't begrudge the cockiness in the least. "In business, and many other things in life, for that matter, one must be prepared to take risks. Roberto knows that. We took a calculated risk in coming all the way out here to get the Topaz. It was really a, how do you say it, a long shot."

Eva interrupted, anxious to get to the point of her question. "But having come all the way here from Paris, don't you feel defeated?"

"Not at all," he went on patiently, his accent soothing her as much as his words. "You see, a calculated risk implies that there will not be a total loss should the risk fail. In this case, *ici,* we have failed in the ultimate objective, but the process of the journey has been of nearly as much merit as that further objective. *Comprenez-vous?"* He made such sense that Eva had to admire him all the more.

"That's a great way of looking at it, Jacques. I guess I hadn't seen it quite like that . . . but you're right! Does Pierre agree with you?"

"In a way. Pierre, as I'm sure you can tell, is a very intense person. He is much more goal-oriented than I. Actually, it's just that I have many subgoals, most of which this trip has satisfied. As for Pierre, perhaps he is disappointed; if so, at least it will take his mind off his other worries." He sent a knowing grin toward her after this last evaluation, then added, "I'd better see what I can do back at the camp. Are you coming?" He rolled down his sleeves, having passably cleaned himself.

As renewed as she felt, Eva was still not ready to face the camp. Shaking her head, she explained, "I'm not quite ready to see it all over again. I think I'll stay here a bit. If someone needs me desperately, you know where I'll be," and she sent him on his way with a smile that relected the fondness she felt for this kind and very sensible man.

When he had disappeared around the bend, Eva lay back on the rock to soak in the few last drying shafts of sunlight. She glanced sideways at the cascading water, its rapid heartbeat the sole sign of the tumult that had been.

Mulling over Jacques's philosophy, she realized just how right he had been. This trip had much to praise it, even without the joy of seeing the Espinhaco Topaz. For much to her amazement, she had indeed been freed of her obsession with Stu, his death, and his family since she had been here. True, she had thought about them, but never with the same mind-possessing pall she had lived with in New York. As heartbreaking as she knew her love for Roberto to be, at least it had reminded her that life still went on, that there was indeed a future.

"You look like Eve in the garden of Eden!" an affectionate note sounded. Eva looked up to see Paul standing there, astonished that he too should have suggested the same analogy that she and Roberto had both made. The uncanniness was furthered when Tom appeared from behind Paul to add, his twinkling eyes teasing her, "Except that you are wearing clothes. . . ."

Eva bounded up, hiding her embarrassment behind a warm grin, to deliver mock clobbers to the heads of the two. "You jokers! Hey, how do you feel, Tom?" she asked, becoming momentarily serious.

"I'm fine, Eva. Just filthy! So if you'll excuse me, I can wash up," he humored her with a wink.

Paul added, "I think you could help Roberto back at the camp." Eva wondered if there was something in his suggestion beyond the mere words, but she chose to overlook it as she waved over her shoulder and headed toward the bend.

She was astounded at the high spirits during supper, even with Jacques's earlier rationalization. She was sure, moreover, that the sugar-cane brandy, called *cachaça* by the Brazilians, which Roberto mysteriously produced from among the supplies, was no bit player in the definitely therapeutic evening. How foresighted he had been to bring along this medicine, Eva acknowledged, feeling the numbing glow of it herself. How much nicer it would have been, though, to have enjoyed it in celebration of a greater success!

The brandy had been definitely called for—it had been very depressing, after they had washed up, to determine bag for bag what had been lost. Eva had lost both her knapsack and her bedroll under the overhang. Miraculously, her camera gear had been hastily stowed with the things on the opposite side of the ruin and was, for the most part, in good working order. Several other bedrolls and knapsacks, not to mention practically all of the digging equipment, had been lost. Roberto readily conceded that it would be impossible to uncover anything more with the few tools that remained.

"This is a democratic expedition," he maintained. "If the majority of you want to try, we try. But it is my judgment that, with the few supplies we have, we have little hope for the gear packed under the hundreds of pounds of earth over there. As for the Topaz, it would take a bulldozer to make much progress toward reaching it now!"

"What do you suggest, Roberto?" Jacques's easy manner came right to the point.

"As much as I hate to say it, I suggest we start back for Terra Vermelho in the morning. We can share clothes, bedrolls, whatever is necessary for the trip back, and we are in good shape for food. Any objections?" His eye scanned the group seated around him, and when no sound of objection was raised, he nodded his head in acknowledgment. It was at that point that the *cachaça* had appeared, and things moved uphill from there.

The evening was indeed a merry one, particularly in light of the day's tragedy. But Eva could understand why. She tried as hard as the next to compensate for the bitter disappointment they all shared, to one extent or another. Having gone through such a trial with these men, she felt closer to all of them tonight, a bond cemented by their mutual ordeal. She drank her share of *cachaça,* soon participating freely in the laughter.

She was unaware of going to bed that night, so strongly had the brandy affected her. Somewhere in her subconscious, she vaguely remembered crawling away from the others, curling up on the ground with a rock as a pillow, and savoring her release from the traumatic day's happenings. Through her haze she sensed some movement around her, some weight bringing warmth to her shoulders, and then nothing.

When she woke up in the morning she was in Roberto's arms. So content had she been, nestled against the warm lines of his body, that she hadn't realized where she was until her head shifted and her ear came to rest against a heartbeat that she knew could not be her own. She bolted up, only to be restrained by the arm that encircled her shoulder. Simultaneously, a hand clapped over her mouth to prevent her outcry, as he motioned with his eyes that the others were sleeping nearby.

It was to her utter dismay that she found herself lying snugly against him, one arm across his chest, legs intertwined. As soon as he was sure that she would be silent, he released her. She promptly disengaged herself from him, snaked out of the sleeping bag—his, she noted, since hers had been buried—and ran quietly to the waterfall to catch her breath.

The sun had not yet come up, but the pale light of dawn provided what little light she needed to find the way to her spot. Splashing cold water on her face, the reality of the situation became clear. She had spent the night with Roberto. What had happened? How had she gotten there? Had anything else happened? She was still dressed in the grimy clothes of yesterday at least that was a good sign. She sat down and buried her face in her hands in embarrassment at her predicament.

It was thus that Roberto found her moments later. He doused his own face with water before coming to sit down next to her. She hadn't looked up yet; she hadn't needed to, to know that it was he who had joined her.

"That was quite a night," he teased, a wicked gleam in his eye.

"Was it?" she replied coldly.

"What do you remember?"

"Not much," she admitted miserably, seeing no point in hiding the truth.

"You didn't have all that much to drink. Do you always react that way to liquor?" He kept his voice soft and peered at her through inquisitive eyes.

"No. Only when I live through torrential rainstorms and landslides!" she retorted sarcastically.

"Ah, I see your sense of humor is returning. Good! Now, tell me what you do remember about last night." His persistence angered her, he was that determined to humiliate her.

"I told you. I don't remember much," she snapped. "I remember lying down, something being thrown over me, and that's about all until I woke up in . . ." she broke off, unable to spell out the source of her mortification.

"In my arms?" He wasn't going to let up on her.

She became more perturbed by the minute. *"You* tell me what happened. One of us must have been aware of what he was doing and it sure wasn't me! What did happen?" she demanded.

His devilish smile irked her even more. "You had no sleeping bag and I did. When you more or less passed out, I put you into mine. Where was I to sleep? You didn't seem to mind a bit when I climbed in with you. In fact, you were very cuddly!" he smirked, but to Eva's greater embarrassment, he hadn't finished.

"I can't say I got much sleep. You nearly drove me crazy, moving next to me so seductively! So you see the sacrifices I make? The least you could do is to thank me!" His mockery was too much for Eva.

"Thank you?" she burst out, then immediately lowered her voice, realizing that the last thing she wanted was for any of the others to know what had taken place.

"Thank you?" she repeated in a harsh whisper. "What should I thank you for? For putting me into your bed with you? You've been wanting to do that since the day I arrived," she accused, her eyes narrowing suspiciously. "Do you always take advantage of helpless women?"

She found his calmness, as he replied, all the more maddening in light of her own agitation. He stated quietly, "I have never taken advantage of you. You've gotten just what you wanted. Can you deny that you slept better last night, next to me, than you have in months?"

"If it hadn't been for your damned brandy," her eyes flashed with her ready response, "I wouldn't have been anywhere near you. You are detestable! Are you so desperate to seduce me that you have to resort to getting me drunk?"

It was with only minor satisfaction that her words finally hit a sensitive cord. He stood up abruptly, grabbed her upper arms with his powerful hands, yanked her to her feet, and pulled her body firmly against his. She had no choice but to look up at him, his eyes blazing with a passion her heart wished were love but her mind knew to be hatred.

His response was calculated, each word spoken with conviction. "No, Eva. When I take you, you'll be stone sober. Lovemaking, in case you didn't know, is an activity involving two people. You, my black widow, will make love to me as passionately as I will to you. And you'll remember every minute of it!" With a final piercing glance, he thrust her away and was gone. Eva could only stagger at his force, her open mouth a token of all the words that hadn't come.

Trembling, she turned back to the waterfall. *When* I take you, he had said. When . . . when . . . she gagged on his presumption. That was, after all, what he wanted. Not her company. Not her help. But her body! *When* I take you, he had said. Of all the . . . she couldn't think of enough derogatory names to use to describe him.

Yet as each one entered and then passed from her mind, she knew that her love for him was as strong as ever. He had been right. She had slept better, in his arms, last night than she had slept in a very long time. She had felt safe, warm, comforted, cared for, and desired. Yes, even the last—desire—was what she needed. She needed to be desired, unfortunately not only in body, as Roberto wanted her, but also in spirit. She had come so close to finding the perfect relationship, she reflected sadly, just as the expedition had come so close to finding the perfect Topaz. The major element lacking in the relationship she saw between herself and Roberto was entirely one-sided, his love.

Well, she rationalized, it was almost over now. They would soon be on the return leg of their journey. By tomorrow they would be back in Terra Vermelho, and as soon as possible after that, she would be on her way to New York. As much as she hated to return there, she feared remaining here more. And anyway, she had her pictures to deliver to her editor.

The aroma of fresh coffee wafted through the trees and around the bend, bidding her return to the scene of the crime. And return she did, avoiding Roberto's gaze and his company. She discovered that the rest of the crew had awaked in her absence, and both packing and breakfast were well under way.

There was something terribly anticlimactic about the

morning. The effects of the brandy were gone, so there were neither high spirits nor the dark of night to hide from view the devastation of the mine collapse. Particularly noticeable in the morning air, once the coffee had been downed, was the odor of wet earth, a dank sort of smell which imprinted itself in Eva's memory, guaranteeing that in the future should she smell a similar odor of moisture, her mind would reflexively return to this mountain side.

Actually, the packing was an abbreviated affair this time around, since well over half of the supplies had either been consumed or entombed. To Eva's surprise and chagrin, Roberto approached her just before they were ready to set off. She tried to head in the opposite direction, but he was too fast for her and cut her off.

"What do you want now?" she demanded uneasily.

"Shhh! Do you want everyone to know about our secret relationship?" he taunted in a low voice.

"That kind of inane question doesn't even deserve an answer. What do you want?" she spat out, trying desperately to keep a stern front under his melting gaze.

To her puzzlement, there was a melancholy look in his eyes at her response. "Your camera bag. We have plenty of room for it on the donkeys. Do you want to pack it up?"

"What? And get out of shape?" She refused to be bought off with empty gestures.

"Hmmm . . . you're right. We wouldn't want that to happen, would we?" he chided, giving her a look from head to toe which left no question as to his meaning.

Before she had time to recover from this visual rape —for that was how she thought of it—he turned from her and headed back to secure the final straps around the animals. Once more, she thought disdainfully, he had gotten the last word.

Within moments they were on their way, retracing

the steps they had so enthusiastically taken but two days before. Eva spared no last glance at the mine, or what had once been the mine. The sight of yesterday's destruction still knotted her stomach, and, given the fact that redeeming the Topaz was now out of the question, she had no desire to linger further.

Her Eden, as she thought of it fondly, was another matter. The early morning sun was now dancing on the shimmering stones in a primitive gavotte. Letting herself fall to the end of the procession, she lifted her camera to capture a few final shots of this, nature's romp. She moved in closer, backed away, shifted to the left, then to the right, knelt down to ground level— snapping her shutter again and again in hopes that maybe one, just one, of her frames would capture the freedom, the happiness, the pure life that this waterfall symbolized for her. She had felt so at peace in this spot; if only she could look at a photograph in the future that would convey a fraction of that same peace, she would be grateful.

Of course, the memories of this waterfall would also include memories of Roberto, his body warm and masculine, his chest firm and electrifying against her own. As painful as these memories might be to her, she knew that she would cherish them always. Even now, flooding back, they sent a thrill of excitement through her.

"Are you going to stand there much longer? You wouldn't want to be lost forever, would you?" He stood so magnificently on the path, arms crossed on his chest, well-muscled legs set confidently, dark eyes staring at her—almost as a living re-creation of her momentary daydream.

Seeing him thus, she couldn't think of any properly sarcastic comment to make. Instead, she made one last exposure, this in token defiance of his implication that she shouldn't stop, slipped the strap of the camera over one shoulder and the strap of the duffel over the other, took one last look, a personal farewell, at the waterfall, and joined him as he turned and proceeded on the path.

"Yes, Roberto. I could be lost here forever. Right by that waterfall. It's so peaceful there . . ." she replied pensively.

"I think you'd get tired of constant serenity. You enjoy a good fight. Your face lights up, your whole body becomes alert. You rise to the challenge each time." There was no mockery in his analysis this time, as they walked side by side, the rest of the party ahead and out of sight.

She couldn't totally deny what he said. He was perceptive once again, she had to admit. "I suppose you're right. I do like a challenge. But there's a difference between a challenge and a battle. Just as I thrive on the challenge, I die a little bit with every battle. There has to be a certain amount of harmony in life—at least, in some aspects of life."

"As in a marriage?" he broke in.

"Yes. As in a marriage." He knew to what she referred, so she didn't elaborate. Although she felt the subject to be verging on the uncomfortable, she was thoroughly enjoying his company, she realized. He was fun to talk with, intelligent, perceptive. She opened up to him readily. More importantly, he seemed to be enjoying himself also. Without the sparring which usually characterized their interchanges, she sought to prolong the conversation.

"There was challenge back at the waterfall," she went on. "Nature always provides a challenge. Look what happened yesterday! But when the storm ends, the cascade always returns to where it was. You can depend on its constancy. I do need the challenge, but I also need the constancy. I guess I'm not as strong as

I'd like to believe." She was amazed at her rambling and shot him a look of self-consciousness at the frankness of her confession.

His eyes caught hers, and the look of compassion they held made her ache inside anew. "It's nothing to be embarrassed about, Eva. I think none of us are as strong as we may think. It's perfectly natural to need others to lean on. That's what binds people together. That's what marriage is all about."

How easy for him to dispassionately philosophize on the need of people for each other, she pondered. If he only knew her need . . . but she was getting too melancholic now. She had to lighten things up a bit.

"Now how would you know about marriage? Aren't you the classic bachelor?" she teased, momentarily diverting her concentration from the path underfoot to his thoughtful eyes. Did he see the hint of sadness that her smile must have betrayed? She prayed not.

"As a 'classic bachelor,' as you so smartly put it, I can all too clearly see what I'm missing. I have needs too, Eva."

How could he be so sincere, she wondered, and then shatter the fragile peace they had built by making reference to his male needs. Typical, she thought, lowering her head even more to avoid his gaze.

They had finally come within sight of the others, and just as Eva had begun to tire under the brisk pace he had set to catch up, she was relieved to be able to end this discussion which, begun so meaningfully, was bound to end in an explosion if carried on much longer. Having nothing more to add in a civil tone, she remained silent. He accepted her withdrawal and moved ahead to see how the leaders of the line fared.

The trek continued with only a noontime stop for lunch and a rest. Eva chatted with the others, but had no further opportunity to talk with Roberto, a mixed blessing.

By midafternoon, the intensity of the heat had begun to affect them all. The pace slowed, for which Eva was grateful, as she had begun to feel the letdown, the anticlimax, of this return trip. She was taken aback when Roberto walked up to her and without a word removed the duffel from her shoulder and put it over his. He must have known she would be too tired to argue, she mused. And she was not about to let her pride stand in the way of his help, especially since she would be leaving tomorrow, out of his life and beyond caring.

But she would care. Every inch of her protested that she would care. The very thought of never seeing Roberto again cast a spell of sadness over her which persisted throughout dinner and the evening, and only dissipated when exhaustion overtook her and she fell into a deep sleep.

As always, the morning brought a feeling of renewal, a putting into perspective of the previous day's quandaries. Eva forced herself to look to the future. She would return to New York, immerse herself in her work, as she had done so often before, and let time do its healing.

Throughout the day's hike, Eva's thoughts returned periodically to this resolution. But by midafternoon, when the familiar sight came into view, the intimate clutter of rooftops in the distance below them, she knew for certain that, just as she would return to New York, a part of her would remain forever in this little town of Terra Vermelho. And that was an aspect of her future with which she would have to somehow learn to cope.

CHAPTER 9

Contrary to her expectation, Eva's spirits lifted significantly once back in Terra Vermelho. She was again shown to the room—Roberto's room, which she had used when she had first arrived. It was only at that point, catching her reflection in the mirror, that she realized how bedraggled she looked and how filthy she felt. A bath was a definite must, she determined.

At the stairs, making her way toward the kitchen in search of Maria, she came upon Roberto who, judging from the clean clothes and towel over his shoulder, had the same idea. He was in an unusually good mood, she noted, wondering off-handedly if he'd had time to pay a visit on his little girl friend yet.

His low voice was friendly. "It looks like I didn't get in there fast enough. You *are* looking for a bath, aren't you?"

Evidently he had made the same deduction. "I was, although I don't know where it is. I was just going to ask Maria to show me. But you go ahead. I'll visit with Maria in the meanwhile. Is she in the kitchen?" Eva found it easy to keep a level head, with Roberto so near, only as long as the conversation remained fairly impersonal.

"When I last saw her she was." His eyes sparkled in amusement. "How do you communicate with her?"

"Oh, a little sign language here and there. She's a friendly sort. A smile says so much with Maria. I'd like some coffee, if it wouldn't be imposing on her." What she really wanted, though she didn't understand why, was some female companionship, conversation or no.

"I'm sure she'd be pleased. Maybe you can give her a hand, anyway. She's making a special dinner for tonight. We'll all be eating together—at about eight?" Again, the mischievous look in his eye. "If you get bored in the kitchen, you could always come converse with me in the bath. . . ."

"Thank you, but no thank you. I'll just have my coffee now and bathe later," she replied, coolly ignoring the impertinence of his suggestion.

"As you wish . . ." he drawled, handsomely appealing even in his dirty state, she conceded. "But if you change your mind, the tub is through the second door on the left. Don't forget!"

Even with his boyishness as put on as it was, Eva had to laugh good-naturedly at him. He could really be so charming at times. Perhaps if he were a little less charming right about now and a little more aggravating, she would not feel such twinges at the prospect of leaving in the morning. As she headed toward the kitchen, her smile faded at that thought.

Sure enough, Maria was working busily in the kitchen. It was the first time Eva had seen her since their return. Looking up in surprise, Maria dropped everything to bustle over and give Eva a warm hug, babbling excitedly in Portuguese. Without having to ask for it, Eva was given a cup of steaming coffee, which she sipped while Maria flitted about at her work. All of Eva's hand motions asking Maria to let her help with something fell on deaf ears; Maria fully understood her but insisted that she sit and rest.

What a delightful person, Eva thought, as Maria efficiently chopped all sorts of thing Eva did not recognize into small pieces. Several pots were already steaming; this would be quite a farewell dinner, Eva judged, from the extravagance of the preparation.

Farewell dinner . . . again the tugging sensation at Eva's stomach. That must have been the explanation for Roberto's good humor. Of course! By tomorrow, he would once again be unencumbered by this house guest. Not that her presence had slowed him down very much, if the memory of that beautiful bronze-skinned girl served her well. But she must be a kind of thorn in his side, resisting his advances as she had. Yes, she was an affront to his male ego, and, as such, he would certainly be glad to see her go.

The frown on Eva's brow had attracted Maria's attention, bringing a look of concern to her cherubic face and setting off a whole new barrage of incomprehensible words. Eva immediately calmed her with an affectionate smile, reclaimed the towel and clothes she had laid on the chair and, indicating to Maria that she was going to bathe, made her way out of the kitchen, down the hall and up the stairs in the direction Roberto had shown.

The bath did wonders for Eva. Gradually, layers of accumulated dirt and sweat dissolved into the water which, hot and steamy, cleansed her as the cold water of her waterfall had simply been unable to do. Her muscles soaked in the relaxing warmth until the warmth had just about gone. Only then did she step out of the tub, dry herself off, and dress, before returning to her room for the little while that remained before dinner.

How good it felt to put on a dress, after days of

wearing the same T-shirt and jeans. She chose, for the evening, a comfortable halter-topped sun dress, of a crisp cotton material, flattering with its slim skirt, open back, plunging vee-neck, and strap that tied around the neck. Its color, a teal blue, emphasized both the green in her eyes and the auburn tinge of her hair. It mattered very much to her that these men, her friends who had seen her at her worst in the soggy muck of the rainstorm, should be left with a memorable impression. Or was it really Roberto whom she wanted to impress?

For whatever reason, she took added care with her makeup, what little she had that had not been lost in her knapsack, and with her hair. The latter she caught up loosely at the back of her head, leaving delicately tumbling tendrils to create an impression of total femininity. That was it, she realized. Having spent the last few days as one of the guys, she wanted, tonight, to look feminine, act feminine, feel feminine, and to be treated as such.

With a final smudge to her blue eyeshadow, Eva left her room to join the men, who would be arriving downstairs just about now.

The evening was, without doubt, one of the highlights of Eva's trip. She suspected that each of the men—yes, even Pierre—had some misgivings about leaving the next day, so the subject was avoided by all. Maria had outdone herself, serving dish after dish of delectable local fare, from a light rice broth with chicken pieces, called *canja,* to a delicious *cozido,* a stew with a myriad of exotic ingredients, to *palmitos,* the tender hearts of palm known to be a Brazilian specialty, to the delightful pastries called *bom cocados,* that were made of coconut.

Throughout the meal Roberto dispensed liberal servings of *batida,* the potent mixture of fruit juice and whiskey which every Brazilian concocted with his own favorite tropical fruit. Eva was careful on this score, not wishing to make a fool of herself with drink a second time, although she needn't have worried. Roberto diligently kept tabs on her, too, and long after he stopped refilling her glass, he was still offering more to the others.

The end of the evening came all too quickly for Eva's liking. The atmosphere had been intimate, the conversation both stimulating and entertaining. The plan was for four of them—all except Roberto and Paul, who were staying on a little longer—to share a taxi into Belo Horizonte the next morning, so there were no immediate good-byes exchanged as each set out for his own place of lodging. When the joviality had died away, there were only Eva and Roberto remaining behind, staring at each other awkwardly across the empty room.

Eva was suddenly acutely aware of Roberto, her love for him and her desire for him. Above all, she knew that she would be leaving tomorrow for the last time. She felt a knot beginning to form in her throat at the thought of never seeing Roberto again, and her eyes filled with tears.

He stood across the room from her, watching her, mindful of the inner torment she was going through. Neither of them moved; neither shifted his gaze from the other. Eva was growing more distraught by the moment, the knot moving from her throat to her stomach and back again, but she could no more tear her gaze from him than she could deny her love.

Slowly, Roberto approached her, stopping several feet away. Eva remained frozen, fighting her personal battle of self-restraint, until he gently held his arms out to her in silent invitation. It was all she needed. She had known all along that she wouldn't have been able to resist. In one forward motion she was in his arms, clinging to his shoulders, burying her head on his chest to smother the sobs she feared would escape.

He stood and held her, the steel band of his arms entrapping her against his long, hard body. Finally, the desire became too great. She lifted her eyes to his face and for an infinitely long moment they remained locked onto his. Slowly, lovingly, her gaze moved over his cheekbone and along his jaw line, settling on his lips in a return invitation. That was all Roberto had needed, as his mouth lowered to hers in a fiery declaration of desire. His lips burned against hers, tasting, exploring, caressing, and then permitting her to satisfy the same devouring need. She sought his tongue as he sought hers, and the deeper kiss touched off a new wave of sensuality.

When Eva paused, breathless, Roberto nuzzled her neck, the sensitive hollow at her throat, her shoulder. She shuddered in excitement, the telltale ache in her loin growing steadily. At that moment, held within Roberto's soul-reaching embrace, she knew that she would not, could not, deny him tonight. She wanted him desperately, even if it had to be for only this one night.

It was, uncannily, as though he sensed some subtle change in her. He raised his mouth from her ear lobe and studied her for a long moment. His gaze tore at her heart such that she could wait no longer. In a husky whisper, she begged, "Please, Roberto . . . love me . . . just for tonight . . ." He kept her waiting no longer.

With one strong sweep, he had lifted her into his arms and was carrying her out of the room, through the hallway, up the stairs, and into her room—his room—that they would share this one night. Her arms were about his neck as he carried her, her face buried in his neck, inhaling the smell of his skin, so warm and fresh and distinctive, intoxicating her with its own brand of liquor.

Gently Roberto laid her on the bed, then sat down next to her. Taking her wrists with his hands, he drew them up over her head, pinning them to the pillow as he leaned over to kiss her again, a slow, tantalizing kiss which only increased the frantic jumping in her stomach.

"You're beautiful, Eva. I need you so much," he murmured softly, as he reached up to remove the pin which held her hair, easing her curls over the pillow in graceful tumbles. Then he lowered himself down next to her on the bed and pulled her onto her side into his embrace. Their lips played, though barely touched, as his hands kneaded her shoulders, then traced the plunging vee of her neckline, before slipping inside the halter to fondle her breast, so full and creamy white. She cried out briefly at his touch, aching for more, wanting nothing short of his full possession.

As Roberto had predicted, she was not to be a passive lover. As his hands sensuously alerted the tips of her breasts to the height of passion, her own had unbuttoned his shirt and were playing on his chest, adoring each curling tuft and every sinewy bulge, reveling in the very touch of his skin. Her insides felt as though they would burst as his thigh thrust between her legs, massaging her, heightening her need even as she felt his.

As his lips took hers once more, his hand left her breast and moved to the hem of her dress, searing a path up her thigh to a height she could bear no longer.

When she cried out this time, it was in sheer pain. The spasms in her stomach had intensified and there was no more mistaking these pains for those of passion.

"Oh, my God, Roberto! Something's wrong!" she cried out as the reality of her condition hit her. Roberto stiffened, then immediately disengaged himself from her and arose from the bed. Tears of pain stung her eyelids as she repeated, gasping in between spasms, "Something's wrong!" Her voice had reached a high pitch of panic at the sudden seizure.

"You little bitch!" returned the low-toned growl, as Roberto glared at her disbelievingly. "I should have known. I should have known," he muttered between his teeth as he slammed out of the room, leaving Eva doubled up on the bed.

She remained in shock where she was for what seemed like an eternity, having neither the strength nor the desire to move from where she lay. With each new spasm the pain grew stronger, tearing through her in excruciating intensity. Her mouth went dry and beads of perspiration broke out on her forehead, as she sought to smother the outcries that threatened to erupt with each renewed cramp.

So preoccupied was she with this sudden physical onslaught that she could only spare an intermittent thought for Roberto, their moment together now lost, and the parting look of hatred in his face. He didn't believe her! He didn't know she was truly sick!

"Roberto . . . Roberto . . ." she murmured over and over between breathless sobs, his name almost a chant that she willed to guide her through whatever this was. If he only knew how much she needed him now, to comfort her and cradle her through the enervating cramping which racked her body.

She didn't understand what was wrong. Her health had always been so good. She was rarely sick. Now, alone and frightened, she let the tears flow freely, rolling down her cheeks uncontrollably, streaking through the rising heat of fever. What was this, she frantically asked herself again. I haven't been sick like this since . . . my God . . . it couldn't be . . . there was no fish in that meal.

Her medicine. If she had accidentally ingested even a small piece of fish, she would need her medicine. A tortured moan escaped from her lips as she realized that the medicine she always carried as a precaution, which she had even brought with her into the mountains, had been crushed and buried under the landslide and would be of no use to her now.

"Roberto! Roberto!" This time she screamed his name, again and again, with every last bit of strength her pain-racked body could gather. Where was he? He would know! That had to be it, she acknowledged hysterically. Fish! She must have eaten fish! She had to get to a doctor! Only too well did she remember the increasingly devastating stomach cramps, the raging fever, the eventual breathing difficulty that accompanied these attacks.

The fever brought with it a dizziness, which fought her as she attempted clumsily to rise from the bed. She had to get help. Someone had to be in the house. Roberto? Maria? Her intention was sidetracked by a suddenly rising nausea; she staggered to the basin on the low table just as the convulsions began, and her badly shaking arms and legs supported her as she lost the contents of her stomach. When the vomiting ceased and she could stand no more, her weakened knees gave way and she sank limply to the floor, grasping her stomach in a fit of renewed pain.

It was here that Maria found her, alerted by her earlier screams. Eva heard the excited babbling in Portuguese before she felt the arms, which gently lifted her to her feet and helped her to the bed. The fever was dulling her sense of purpose; she had to break through.

"Maria, fish . . . was there any fish in the dinner?" she begged, grabbing Maria's arms and raising panicky eyes to hers. "Fish," she repeated, "I'm allergic to fish! Please . . . tell me . . ." Her voice broke off as even her fevered brain knew that Maria couldn't understand, and she sank down on the bed, drained by the frantic exertion.

Maria's deft hands quickly stripped her sun dress from her and bathed her burning skin. Eva couldn't resist, her limbs were so weakened and her mind so hazy. She passed in and out of a shallow consciousness, at each moment of lucidity calling Roberto's name, pleading with Maria to get him.

Her stomach churned again, and this time Maria held her head as the involuntary convulsions shook her. Patiently, all the while crooning soothing Portuguese words to her, Maria cleaned her and changed her clothes again, this time putting her into one of Roberto's shirts, pulled from the tall dresser. The ashen color of her face, broken only by a few small spots of fever, was as white as the shirt, which swam about her shoulders and fell to her thighs.

Again and again she called his name, only to find that it was Maria's cooling hand on her forehead . . . Maria, who couldn't understand that she needed something stronger than cold compresses.

Eva didn't hear the door open. She was in a moment of delirium, back in the mountains, in her own Eden. The next spasm of pain brought her around, though, and she opened her fever-glazed eyes to see Roberto standing by the bed. She completely missed the fear in his eyes as he gazed upon her pale and fevered features, so intent was she in conveying the message she was grasping to remember.

"Roberto . . . help me . . . Roberto . . ." she shrieked in a high-pitched tone

Roberto interrupted her, as he sat down and took her hot hand in his. "Shhh . . . just rest. You need to sleep." She couldn't make out the look on his face through the blur of tears in her own eyes.

"No, Roberto . . . fish . . . I'm allergic to fish. Did we have any fish in the dinner? I only get sick like this when . . ." she broke off, a new surge of cramping silencing her. She rolled in agony onto her side and tucked her knees up to ease the pain.

Roberto stroked her hair as he turned to say something in Portuguese to Maria. His tone was calm, though grim, when he spoke close to Eva's ear. "Yes, there was a small amount of fish in the stew. What are you supposed to do? You must have some medicine . . . just tell me and I can get it."

"I always carry it. It was in my knapsack . . . buried," she cried out hysterically. Nothing else needed to be said. Roberto instantly gathered Eva's slim body to him, lifted her from the bed and headed for the door as he called instructions over his shoulder to Maria.

Once in his arms, Eva relinquished the burden of the responsibility to him, knowing that she would trust him to make whatever decisions needed to be made. The wave of consciousness ebbed and flowed. Eva felt herself being put into Roberto's four-wheel drive. She felt him climb into the driver's seat and pull her against him, protectively secured by his right arm, as he started the car with his left.

She asked no questions. Roberto spoke softly, calmly, every now and then, as they drove through the wee-hour darkness, explaining that there was an excellent hospital in Belo Horizonte, where they were headed, assuring her that everything would be all right.

At one point the pain became too great and she cried out. He pulled her even closer to him, as though to absorb the pain himself and thus ease hers. "It's all right, honey. You'll be all right. It won't be very long now. Hang in there for me!"

How fast he drove she neither knew nor cared. Her breathing grew increasingly labored during the long drive, and she was struggling for air by the time the bright lights of the emergency exit came into view. Roberto pulled to an abrupt stop, jumped out of the vehicle, gently pulling Eva around the steering wheel and into his arms, as he bolted into the hospital.

If the events of the last few hours were a dim haze, even more so were those of the next few hours. Eva's consciousness glimpsed the flurry of activity from afar, coming and going through the swirling mists of fever. Low voices conversed about her, probing hands examined her, able fingers secured an oxygen mask over her nose and mouth. Faces came and went, orders flowed. Eva felt herself being turned and the lifesaving injection being given, and almost instantly the cramping eased. When she mustered enough strength to open her eyes, she saw only Roberto, keeping a silent vigil at her side, his eyes never leaving hers, his hand never releasing hers. Her lids lowered again in exhaustion, Roberto's nearness imprinted on her ephemeral consciousness.

Her body quieted as she slept, the violent spasms receding, her breathing steady once again. As the light of dawn filtered through the window, she awoke with a start, one last tremor twisting at her stomach before passing from her. Roberto was there. "Shhh. Sleep, baby. I'm here."

He had to lean closer to hear her faint whisper. "Don't leave me, Roberto." She turned pleading eyes to him briefly, before sinking again to the depths of unconscious sleep.

He never left her. He was there when one nurse removed the oxygen. He was there when another bathed her spent body. He was there when the doctor re-examined her and administered a second injection. He dozed occasionally in his chair, having slept not at all that night, but he never let go of her hand.

By the late morning she was out of danger, as she had known she would be with proper medication, and had fallen into a deep and restful sleep. It was several hours later when she fully gained consciousness, open-her eyes to find Roberto's, dark and clear, gazing at her.

He smiled, so warmly that her heart turned over. "How do you feel?" he asked in a velvety voice, his smile offsetting the fatigue etched into the rest of his face.

She was weak, though entirely lucid now. "Much better." She paused, her eyes never straying from him, before continuing in a shaky voice. "Thank you for staying with me. I was terrified when I realized I didn't have my medicine—I'm usually so careful."

Roberto's finger went to her lips to silence them, remaining a moment too long in its feathery touch, before he quickly withdrew it. "Shhh. It's all over now. You'll be fine."

"When can I leave the hospital?"

"The doctor says that you'll need several more shots. And he'd like to keep you overnight just to make sure that you can keep food down. You gave us all quite a scare." Again the warm, affectionate smile that Eva adored.

She looked away from him then, her mind returning to the night before. In a timid voice she began, "Roberto? I'm sorry . . ." She looked at him as she finished, wanting him to know her sincerity. "I'm sorry . . . about last night. I didn't mean to back out . . ."

The sadness in his eyes matched hers, as he smiled gently at her and said nothing. She knew that her one chance was gone. Her body had betrayed itself. She dozed off again, as much in escape from her heart-rending thoughts as in cure of her fever-scourged being.

When she awoke it was supper time, and Roberto

was just finishing some food he'd been brought. He looked better having eaten, though he was still exhausted. Eva felt well enough herself to worry about him.

"You should get some rest," she urged. "Where can you get some sleep?"

"There's a hotel down the street. I'll take a room later. How do you feel?" he asked, his eyes scrutinizing her.

"I really feel fine . . . just weak. That's the way it always is," she added with resignation.

"Does this sort of thing happen often?" he asked skeptically, one eyebrow raising humorously.

"No. Not since I was a child. When I got angry at my parents I'd eat fish." She blushed in embarrassment. "It would punish them but good! Unfortunately, it punished me as well," she laughed.

"Now there's some color in your cheeks. You look better!" His dark eyes twinkled at her, and with his head cocked at an appealing angle and his thick hair falling casually across his forehead, she could have hugged him. Instead, she quickly looked away so as not to foist on him her unsolicited affection.

At that moment a familiar face peered around the edge of the partially opened door. "So this is where you two have been hiding!" burst out the genial voice, and Paul strode into the room, a broad grin on his face.

Eva flinched imperceptibly at the subtle implication of his words, but she couldn't restrain a smile at the sight of his friendly expression. Oblivious to her discomfort, Paul went on.

"We were pretty surprised to arrive for breakfast this morning and find that you had taken off for the night." Now he must have caught the darkening in Roberto's face, which Eva clearly saw at a glance, for he deftly smoothed the rough edges by turning his attention solely to her. "How are you feeling, Eva? I understand you were quite sick!"

Eva needed some lightening up after the look at Roberto's expression moments earlier. "Now how would you know that? How do *you* talk with Maria? Tell me your secret," she teased with genuine curiosity.

It worked. Both Paul and Roberto laughed at her question, exchanging mischievous winks at the same time. How alike they were, Eva thought once again.

"So you've had trouble, eh? I know exactly what you've gone through. As for me, on the day that I received raw steak with my eggs, I decided to pick up a little Portuguese. Just a few words. They've served me well, at least as far as Maria is concerned. You should try it!" He laughed again.

"I would," she replied sincerely, "but since I'll be leaving soon, that problem will solve itself." Now she had done it herself! Oh, yes, that particular problem may be solved upon her departure, but another will only be beginning! A cold shudder passed through her, and Roberto immediately became alert.

"Are you all right?" he asked formally.

"Yes . . . yes . . . just a leftover spasm, I guess," she excused herself quickly. A brief look at Roberto was enough to see the impatience in his eyes.

Paul saved her. "What happened, Eva? Maria babbled something about fish, but my Portuguese isn't *that* good. When did you take sick?"

Poor Paul, moaned Eva to herself. If he only knew what he was asking! She didn't dare look at Roberto as she answered. "Last night, maybe an hour or so after you all left, it hit. I've been allergic to fish since childhood, and unfortunately, I didn't know there was any in the stew. To complicate matters, the medicine I always carry was buried in the landslide—it had been in my knapsack—and by the time I realized what was wrong, I was pretty far gone. However, I'm fine now, as you can see. Modern medicine does wonders!" She smiled her strongest smile to convince him, and herself. "What brings you down here?" she continued.

"I saw Tom off about an hour ago. Pierre and Jacques flew out earlier. They were sorry to have missed you. They send their best." Again the descent of an ominous cloud into the atmosphere. Eva felt her insides churn, partly in disappointment at not being able to say good-bye to the three, partly in anticipation of her own departure. Despite her own discomfort she realized that Roberto had been unusually silent during the conversation. Looking over at him, she caught him glowering at her with an intensity that tore into her. She had to think quickly.

"Roberto, now that Paul is here, you don't really have to stay. Maybe you want to get some rest . . ." It was the last thing she wanted to say. But having sensed his growing tension, it was the lesser of the evils. It hurt her more to feel his distaste for her than to ask him to leave. Up until Paul had arrived, they had existed in a kind of limbo, with no reminders of past enmity. His arrival had, however, brought back the stark reality of the situation. As kind as Roberto had been to her since she had been sick, she knew that it was only sympathy for her predicament, and a lingering sense of responsibility for her as a member of the team, which had kept him so close. The luxury of having him near her had to end somewhere. Paul might be able to cheer her, if that was at all possible.

"I'll stay for a few more minutes to make sure Paul doesn't tire you," he replied gruffly, "and then we'll both find some place to sleep." His tone relaxed a little as he turned to Paul. "You took a taxi in with the others? Then stay here tonight and we'll go back to Terra Vermelho tomorrow morning."

Paul smiled affectionately. "I was hoping you'd say that. It's not fair for you to have Eva all to yourself, you know!" He flushed faintly, realizing that he had unintentionally put his foot in his mouth again. He rushed on, searching the room with his eyes. "Where's your camera, Eva? I thought photographers took advantage of every possible situation to get a picture!"

She smiled somewhat ruefully. "I guess I'm not *that* much of a professional. When the action stirs up, I get too involved in what's happening to think about taking pictures. It's only afterward that I realize the terrific shots I've missed!"

"I can't blame you. I think I'd be the same way! It takes a certain amount of ruthlessness to be able to carry on as usual during tragedies, or near ones," Paul added, understanding as always, "and you aren't a ruthless person!"

She shrugged modestly at the subtle compliment, stealing a sideways glance at Roberto, who was eyeing her intently, before replying to Paul. "Oh, I don't know. I surprise myself sometimes at the things I photograph. But there was no way, for example, that I could have been able to photograph the landslide the other day. I didn't even stop to wonder where my camera was until the whole thing was over! And as for last night, well, I was pretty out of it." She flushed, again looking to Roberto for some response. The only one she received was an angry frown which immediately drained all pleasure from the conversation, from her point of view.

"I guess I'll never win a Pulitzer as a photojournalist," she finished, suddenly feeling tired again. Mercifully, Roberto picked up on her mood.

He rose, turned to Paul with instructions, and said tensely, "I'm going to speak to the doctor. Stay here with Eva until I get back, then we'll go. I won't be long." Without a further look at Eva, he left the room, a heavy silence descending in his wake.

Paul looked at Eva, who had closed her eyes and turned her head away from him. Even though he knew her feelings about Roberto, she didn't want him to see the extent of the hurt she felt. But, like his brother, he was too perceptive for her.

"Does it hurt that much, Eva?" he asked softly, as he sat down on the side of the bed.

She remained as she was for a long minute, until she was betrayed by the tears which seeped from under her closed lids to slide onto her cheeks. Unable to speak, she nodded in affirmative response, throwing her arm across her eyes to salvage whatever dignity she could.

Paul's gentle hands reached to her shoulders and pulled her against him, stroking her hair soothingly as she gave way to the quiet weeping. She held onto him, absorbing his comfort, until she gained control of herself enough to draw away from him and lie down against the pillow.

"Maybe you'd better wait outside for him, Paul. I don't want him to see me like this. He'll know right away!" She turned teary eyes to his in silent pleading. "Tell him I've fallen asleep. I really do feel tired."

Then she mustered one final spurt of energy. "Paul," she began in a tremulous voice, "Promise me one thing? Please don't tell him . . . about my . . . problem." She couldn't quite get herself to verbalize her love. "It is *my* problem. It will be hard enough leaving here as it is, but I don't think I could stand his pity." She implored him, "Promise?"

He searched her face intently for several moments, and Eva feared that he might refuse her. Finally, in a voice strangely sad, he agreed. "Sure, Eva. And don't worry. Things work out!" He smiled at her as he smoothed her curls away from her face once more and kissed her on the forehead in a brotherly manner before going out into the hall to intercept Roberto.

Eva did not see either Roberto or Paul again that evening. The nurses made up for the absence by indulgently doting on her. She was brought some weak broth, the first food of any kind she had eaten since that fateful dinner. She was bathed. She was given a rubdown. The doctor visited her again, and she received, much to her relief, the final injection she would need.

She couldn't converse with most of her caretakers. The doctor in charge, as well as one of the nurses, did speak some fragmented English, but otherwise it was the interchange of facial expressions, hand motions, and alien words to which she was becoming quite accustomed.

She slept well that night. By the time she awoke the next morning, the sun was pouring into the room. It was the first time in quite a few days, mused Eva, that she had missed the dawn! Her body was back to normal, albeit a trifle weak. The doctors gave her a clean bill of health, and she was allowed a shower, much to her pleasure. The nurse on watch served her a huge breakfast, and then stood by as she ate every bit.

It was by now midmorning, and she had little to do but wait for Roberto to arrive to pick her up. Getting out of bed, she put on the thin robe over her hospital gown, and stood by the window to soak in the rays of the sun. Even through the pallor which had accompanied her illness, a pink-golden tan shone on her previously wintery pale skin, the physical brand of the fireball which had beaten down on the mountain passes.

Eva could see, even now, the mountains off in the distance. How fresh and inviting they looked, cloaked in the graceful haze of morning. She would miss them when she returned to New York. She would miss this clear air and, yes, its frequently oppressive heat. She would miss the people she'd come to know during the past week. She resolved to visit Paul and Tom in Boston at some point. Maybe . . .

"Feeling better?" his voice was smooth, low, and velvety, as Eva twirled around to face him, marveling at how dashingly handsome he looked, freshly showered and shaven, even wearing the same clothes he had worn since the start of this ordeal.

"I'm fine," she smiled, conscious of how simple she must look in the skimpy hospital robe. But, after all, she had no clothes with her here. As though reading her thoughts, Roberto held out a large bag which had been tucked under his arm.

"Here. I thought you might be able to use these. As ravishing as you look in my shirt, it won't do for you to drive back to Terra Vermelho in broad daylight." Eva blushed as he went on. "I hope the sizes are right. These will help replace the ones you lost."

She looked at him in surprise at his consideration. "Thank you," she replied softly. "It really wasn't necessary." She noticed that his disposition had improved dramatically since last night and assumed that some company more pleasing had revived him.

"To the contrary. It certainly was necessary. That shirt didn't hide an awful lot—I'm not sure I want that kind of temptation today," he drawled at her in amusement. Whatever he did do last night, thought Eva, certainly had returned his mind to its typical track.

Suddenly angry at the jealousy bristling within her at some unknown evening's entertainment, Eva reached over and took the bag, snapping, "If it bothered you so much, you should instruct Maria to be less generous with your clothes. If you'll recall, I had other things on my mind at the time." As further sign of her recuperation, her own penchant for sarcasm had returned.

He appreciated the improvement in her fighting spirit, judging from the grin on his face as he stood, arms crossed on his chest in his typical stance. "If you get dressed, we can be on our way," he suggested, the faintest glint of sensuousness in his eyes.

"If you leave, I can get dressed!" she retorted, not sure how far she could trust either him or herself, and not feeling quite up to the test.

Roberto's gaze bore into hers, a continuing glimmer in their black depths. "As you wish. I'll be right outside the door if you should want me . . ." he invited, his smile mocking her modesty.

She waited until the door was firmly closed behind him before she removed the hospital garb and put on the new clothes he had brought. He guessed her size perfectly, choosing some blue jeans and a pink cotton shirt almost identical in its western style to those he always wore. He had even bought a pair of loafer-type moccasins of the magnificent Brazilian leather Eva had often heard of.

Looking at her image in the mirror, she had to admit to being pleased, illness or no illness. This trip had certainly changed her outward appearance almost as much as her inner one. With her gentle tan, these new clothes, and a strange air of maturity which she had never noticed before, she almost felt up to tackling New York again. What about Roberto? Her inner appearance would never be the same having known him, of that she was certain. With this thought fresh in her mind, an attitude of melancholy swallowed her as she headed for the door, Roberto, Terra Vermelho, and, finally, home.

CHAPTER 10

Eva stood looking down at her opened suitcase, her mind on anything but the packing ahead of her. She still reeled from Roberto's absence. He had been so close to her during her illness. Now, to be deprived of his presence was tantamount to a cold-turkey withdrawal from a binding addiction.

That she was addicted to him she had known since the first day she laid eyes on him at the airport, when she had been immobilized by his gaze. Since the day in the mountains when she realized she loved him, she had known that the relationship was ill-fated. She knew that he could never love her, that she wasn't able to make him love her any more than she had been able to satisfy Stu. The difference between the two situations was that she loved Roberto to distraction.

Roberto had totally enthralled her. She loved the sight of him, the feel of him, the very smell of him. She loved his forcefulness and his decisiveness. She loved the tenderness he could show, as well as the violence that could shake him. No, she had known all along he couldn't love her, but that didn't ease the pain she now felt.

She had even been prepared to give herself totally to Roberto that last night. Indeed, she would have made love to him willingly given the chance, for she knew that she would always treasure the memory of that lovemaking, even having to live the rest of her life without him. But it wasn't to be.

In a perverted kind of way, she had enjoyed being so sick, knowing that Roberto was with her, protectively cradling her, holding her hand, stroking her hair. If it was possible, she loved him more now, after her ordeal, than she had before. That was why she knew she was now doing the right thing.

When she had been discharged from the hospital the day before, it was with a refill of the medicine (which had been lost in the landslide) and with strict orders for the much-needed rest to return her strength. The ride back to Terra Vermelho, though long and tiring for Eva in her depleted state, had been innocuous enough, Paul's presence preventing any confrontation between her and Roberto, who had kept brooding eyes on the road for most of the trip.

The last time she had seen him had been yesterday afternoon, after their return, when she had been properly installed in the large bed upstairs and he had ordered her to sleep. She had done just that; when she awoke, he was gone.

Maria had brought her a simple supper—what little she could eat—and had fussed around her in an endearing way. She was an angel, Maria was, fluffing pillows, neatening the bed, presenting all of her clothes freshly washed and folded. Although they were still unable to communicate verbally, they could understand one another with expressions and gestures. And Maria, throughout her gentle ministrations, had chatted on and on in the nasal flow of the language which Eva would have readily learned, given the excuse.

Despite Eva's protestations, Maria insisted on breakfast in bed this morning. She flitted around like a mother hen while Eva picked at the food, the former assuming that the lack of appetite was still due to her illness. Eva knew otherwise. Roberto's absence was devastating her, heart and soul, even as her body recuperated from its own devastation.

Since she had received the injections at the hospital and the fever had died, Eva no longer had the cloud of delirium to hide within. Rather, her mind had become more and more lucid and she was more and more aware of what had happened to her. Now she had spent the better part of the last twelve hours brooding about Roberto, the strength of her love for him and the absence of his love for her.

Her rational being told her that he had been unable to stay with her any longer than he had. She had certainly been aware of his growing impatience and the increasing tension within him, once she had passed safely out of danger in the hospital. His duty had been satisfied when he saw her back to Terra Vermelho. He must have been only too glad to escape into the arms of some paramour, after long hours of boredom by her sickbed. Her mind told her he would have to break away, even as her heart prayed otherwise. But to no avail. She had lost him. Of that she was sure. Yes, she repeated, the only course left to her was the one she was taking.

She had her return plane ticket to New York. She would pack now and take a taxi to Belo that afternoon. If she was lucky, she thought, she would miss Roberto entirely and thus spare herself an even greater pain than the one already gnawing at her.

As she placed each item of clothing, so thoughtfully

laundered by Maria, back into her suitcase, she lingered on the thoughts which flooded back with them. She would never be the same, she knew. It would be a long time before she could look at that T-shirt and jeans without recalling the mountains, the mine, and, particularly, the man who had been there through it all. She would have to pack these things away to avoid the tormenting memories; but then, she didn't really have much use for them at home, anyway.

Home. Where was home? New York? Yes, she had a home, actually two in New York. But they weren't "home" to her. This isolated Brazilian village seemed more of a home to her now, this charming little two-storied lime-washed cottage with its functionalism and its intimacy meant more to her than her luxurious country house in upstate New York would ever mean. She could stay here, forever, and be perfectly happy, away from the high pressure and hustle of the big city. Especially if Roberto were here . . .

Roberto . . . her heart ached at the thought of him. She wandered over to the window and stood gazing out at the mountains that had given her such solace. Her mind was miles away, in those mountains, by a waterfall, in Roberto's embrace. She was oblivious to all else as she permitted herself this one last mental indulgence. She made no effort to deny the tears beginning to gather, tears of a love found so briefly then lost forever.

The daydream was shattered by the sound of footsteps thundering up the stairs and the door to her room bursting open in a sudden explosion. Eva jerked around in surprise, her tear-misted eyes riveting toward the dark form which stood in the doorway, an image of simmering violence.

"What in the hell do you think you're doing?" the voice bellowed at her, as the towering figure stepped into the room, slamming the door behind him with such force that Eva felt its impact from where she stood. Before she could muster an answer, the angry interrogation continued. "I told you to rest. What's this? Haven't you put me through enough yet? Where in the hell do you think you're going?"

Two coal-black pits glared into the tear-filled green orbs that regarded him now with an unfathomable sadness. Her voice, when it finally came out, was barely more than a whisper. "I have to go, Roberto. I have to go . . ." she trailed off, lowering her head in defeat as the tears fell.

"What do you mean you have to go? You don't have to do anything you don't want to. Isn't that what you keep telling me?" he growled, though the force of his anger had blunted somewhat. "Isn't it?" he repeated, crossing the room to stand before her, demanding an answer.

Without looking at him, Eva nodded in agreement. Why was he punishing her this way? Couldn't he see she was in enough misery?

"Please leave me alone, Roberto. Just go away!" she begged.

"No!" he boomed back. "Not until I get some explanations. Just where in the hell are you going?"

Trying to show a determination she did not possess, Eva turned to the bed and began putting the last of her things into her suitcase. "I'm going back to New York. The expedition's over. I've got to get back. That was the plan all along," she added.

Before she knew what was happening, he was by her side, tearing the clothes out of her hands and throwing them back onto the bed. Then he grabbed her shoulders and spun her around to face him, roughly shaking her as he did so. "I've had enough of your sarcasm, Eva. I want some straight answers for a change!"

He had provoked her once again, and as distraught as she was, Eva wouldn't let it pass. Her anger seethed, "I've always given you straight answers, which is more that I can say for you! And as for my sarcasm, you deserve every bit of it and more for what you've done to me!" The words were out, to her horror; she couldn't retract them now even though it was the last discussion she had ever wanted to have with Roberto. What a stupid fool she was; now she would have to face his further probing.

There was a long silence before Roberto spoke. He had dropped his hands from Eva's shoulders and moved back to lean against the window frame. His stance, usually so casual, was tense now, physically hurt by her last statement, a reaction totally unexpected in a man of his confidence, she thought. Now, when he finally did speak, it was in a tone drained of all anger.

"What do you mean . . . what I've done to you?" His eyes never left her face as he awaited an answer.

Eva knew she'd have to come up with something. She didn't want to confess that he'd made her fall in love with him—she had done that all by herself. Instead, she blurted out defensively, "You've taunted me since I got here with suggestive looks and words. You've insulted me right and left, accusing me of looking for fast fun after my husband's sudden death. You have put me down as being unable to take care of myself . . ." She knew there was a bit of truth in that last one, after the mess she'd made of the last few days.

"I suppose you're right," he admitted softly, much to Eva's surprise. "I have been rough on you," the tenderness in his voice tugging at her hopelessly, "but you asked for it. Showing up the way you did, staring at me with those captivating green eyes of yours, looking so damned beautiful all the time!" The hint of huskiness which Eva knew so well was in his voice and she bristled in self-defense.

"Don't, Roberto!" she screamed, putting her hands to her ears to block out his words. "I can't take it now. Please leave me alone! Don't you see, you're doing it to me again!"

"Doing what?" his voice came back, calm and clear.

"Trying to seduce me! Please stop! I can't fight you, Roberto. Just let me leave!" she begged, tears once again streaming down her face.

Silently he approached her, raising his hands to her face, gently wiping away her tears with his thumbs. "Is that what you thought I was doing? Trying to seduce you? You fool, I've spent most of the last week trying *not* to seduce you! Can't you see that?"

The tenderness in his voice was too much for her. The touch of his hands on her face had begun the stirrings within her. She shook her head in denial of his words, whispering, "It's happening again . . . ," as she raised pleading eyes to his. Every last bit of reason fought back the impulse to fling her arms around his neck, invite his kisses, to give herself totally to him. Resist, she ordered herself one last time! She broke away from his light grasp and moved to the window. The sight of the mountains soothed her, as she knew they would, giving her the strength to finally tell him the truth. Softly, she began, keeping her back to him.

"When I first came here, I only knew I had to get away from New York. I couldn't think there; I was unable to put the pieces of my life back together. Then I saw you at the airport and something moved inside me. It kept growing and growing, each time I saw you. Even when I hated you for what you said and did to me, it kept growing. Then, up in the mountains, I couldn't deny it any longer. I knew what I felt would only hurt me in the end just as it's doing right now. I knew I had no business even looking at a man as I looked at you, with my husband so recently dead. I couldn't help myself, Roberto. I didn't want it to happen. Please believe me." Choked with emotion, she could say no more, but put her fist to her mouth to prevent further release of the anguish she suffered.

The room was so quiet that Eva had begun to wonder whether Roberto had left, when the sound of his footsteps nearing her sent a tremor through her. It was all out now, she thought. He could see for himself what a fool she had been! Maybe now he would leave her alone to her private misery.

With her back to him and her teary eyes downcast, she couldn't see the sparkle that had come to his dark eyes and the softening of features which moments before had been stern and drenched with fury.

"Do you know what you want, Eva?" he asked with a tenderness and, indeed, a vulnerability which took her by surprise.

She turned to face him now, raising still-moist eyes to his with utter conviction. Her voice, a pleading whisper, came from the very depth of her heart.

"I want you to love me . . . as much as I love you . . ." she broke off, abruptly lowering her head in humiliation, no longer able to face him. Quietly and totally beyond her control, the tears burst out afresh and her body was racked by silent sobs of a deep and searing pain.

Roberto's tone was so low that Eva didn't catch his words at first. "I do, Eva! Oh, I do!" he murmured, a slight catch in the usual steadiness of his voice. Slowly, she raised her head in disbelief. The face which gazed at her held none of the disdain, mockery, or even self-assurance she had expected. Rather, she saw eyes that mirrored the same love, the same self-inflicted anguish, the same need which were in hers.

Her astonishment was too much for Roberto. He burst out in a laugh of relief, amusement, and pure emotion. When he stopped, he gently took her face in his hands and brushed her forehead with his lips.

"You little fool! Can't you see that I do love you? I love you more than I could have believed it possible to love anyone."

Suddenly, the tears were of happiness as Eva threw her arms around Roberto's neck and pleaded, "Hold me, Roberto . . . just hold me!"

The force of his arms, the strength of his body, the beating of his heart confirmed his words for Eva. They stood, with the midday sun pouring into the room, indeed into their hearts. They clung to each other as though for life. Eva needed no further assurance than this. Yes, she had been a fool, but in a totally different way than she had previously thought.

Roberto's embrace had lifted Eva to her toes. When the sobs had subsided, he gently lowered her, drawing himself away so that he could look into her face. He slowly bent to kiss away the remaining tears from her eyelids and cheeks, before capturing her lips in a tender declaration of love which rippled through every inch of her. She returned his kiss with an eagerness to give and to proclaim the love she had previously hidden from him.

When their lips reluctantly parted, Roberto drew her down onto the bed next to him, his arm encompassing her body and imprisoning her delightfully against his own warm torso. As they gazed at the mountains, which seemed to have the same effect on him as on her, he began to speak, determination growing with each word.

"I, too, felt something at the airport that day. I didn't know who you were, but I somehow knew you were special. You had a purposefulness about you, a sense of dedication. I could immediately see that there was much to discover within that beautiful shell. The challenge in your eyes excited me. The trouble began when I found you up here in my bed, and I assumed the worst, like a fool . . ."

"No, Roberto," she broke in, only to be silenced by a finger to her lips.

"Yes. It needs to be said, Eva." He spoke with an anger she knew now to be directed against himself, not her. "I did think that you were either out for a good time with a group of men, or a real fortune hunter. Oh, I soon realized how wrong I was, but by that time I was sure you hated me. We always seemed to end up fighting."

"It was my own paranoia," interrupted Eva. "I was sure you were the type to take whatever you could get from a woman!" The twinkle in her eye took the edge off her words.

He looked down at her lovingly as he answered her softly. "Maybe I was, until I met you. Don't mistake me . . . I've wanted you from the start. It's been one cold shower after the other. You looked so tempting, even covered with dust and sweat out there in the hills. But once I realized that you held so much more, I knew I couldn't make a one- or two- or even three-night stand out of an affair with you. I couldn't treat you like a passing body. I know only too well the pain that can cause. . . ."

His voice had grown serious, and Eva sensed the same mystery she had felt at other times. But this was a time for truth. "What do you mean, Roberto?" she prodded gently.

He hesitated, a look of pain on his face, as he began.

"My mother. She and my father met when he was in the States on business. He fell in love with her and she was deeply attracted to him, even though she was engaged to marry someone else. They had an affair. My father wanted to marry her, but she refused. Soon after he returned to Brazil, she discovered she was pregnant. So she postponed her marriage, came down here to give birth to the baby, and then returned to the States alone to marry her fiancé." Here he paused, and Eva understood the resentfulness he had felt as a child toward his mother.

"Didn't she visit you?" she asked in disbelief, finding it unimaginable that a mother could abandon a child thus.

"Not at first. My father had sole custody of me. By the time I was eight she could no longer keep the distance. Part of her was in me and it tore her apart not to know me. She was pulled in two directions at once, between me and her husband, and the suffering grew and grew until she realized that she didn't have to choose between us. They arranged to have me spend vacations with her. It was only when I saw her and lived with her that I could understand why she hadn't married my father. She was a totally different kind of person than he was and lived a completely different kind of life. She was deeply in love with her husband." His brief story completed, he turned to Eva.

"You see, Eva, I didn't want history to repeat itself. My father lived in torment without the woman he loved and seeing my face, a tangible reminder of all he might have had, made it no easier. He and I always had a very tentative relationship for that reason," he explained sadly. "I fought with myself against falling in love with you. Yet, I felt too much for you to risk hurting us both, as my parents did, by having an affair. I knew that I had to make you love me, really love me, but I didn't seem to know how. As well as I manage my business affairs, I was totally unable to manage you. It tore me apart!" He lowered his head, seemingly embarrassed by the confession he was about to make.

"I became jealous of everything you did. I was jealous of Tom when he joked with you, Jacques when he charmed you, even Paulo when he took you under his wing. I was jealous of poor Stuart. I believed at one point that you would mourn him forever; how could I compete with a ghost? And I was jealous of your camera, which you caress so lovingly!"

They laughed in harmony with one another. "Even though you're both dark and handsome, I'll take your body over my camera's any day!" Eva teased, both arms around him hugging his chest as they sat. "No wonder you were such an ogre at times!"

He countered with mock anger, "It was all your fault. You and your stubbornness . . . insisting on coming along to tempt me, fighting to enter the mine when I knew it wasn't safe . . . you drove me to distraction and I couldn't do anything about it." He grinned down at her in his endearing fashion.

But Eva was not so carried away as to forget the insecurities plaguing her. Roberto caught the flicker of doubt that entered her gaze. "What is it, Eva? Everything on the table, now!" he ordered.

"Roberto, I don't know if I am good for you. I failed miserably once before. That's what haunts me, not Stu. What if you get tired of me? I'm not a jet setter. I can't compete with the kind of girls you've been used to. What about them, Roberto? I've been sick with jealousy since I awoke and found you gone yesterday. I imagined you in some other woman's arms and it devastated me. You're a handsome man. Women

—184—

flock to you. Won't they always tempt you?" she asked timidly.

"Eva, do you remember the stewardess you saw me with at the Belo airport that first day? We went out for a drink, but I couldn't see her face for the image of you branded on my mind. I can't look at anyone else now, at least not in the way you refer to. Besides, you just said it yourself. You can't compete with the girls I've been used to. You are in a class by yourself. You don't have to compete." He paused to emphasize his point with a hug before continuing.

"As to where I was yesterday and this morning, I made a quick trip back to Belo to pay an urgent visit to a jeweler friend of mine." His eyes sparkled as he reached mysteriously into his pocket. "He was very annoyed with me when I demanded he carve this on the spot, but he did it." He had withdrawn a chain from which dangled an exquisitely cut stone, of a golden color Eva recognized immediately.

She gasped, "The topaz!" as he nodded in confirmation. The pendant was etched in the shape of a clenched fist with its thumb sticking up between the first and second fingers.

As Eva admiringly touched the crystal, Roberto explained, "It's a figa, a Brazilian amulet meant to ward off evil spirits and to bring good luck, passion, and fertility. You must wear it always and never lose it, or all the evils that have been warded off will besiege you."

"It's magnificent, Roberto! How can I ever thank you?" she exclaimed, as he secured the clasp around her neck and let the amulet rest delicately on her chest.

"You can thank me by letting the figa do its work. It is meant to ward off envy and jealousy. You must forget what's happened in the past. You are the woman I love, the woman I want to marry. You give meaning to my life. Will you marry me, Eva?" It was a proposal from the heart, and Eva's eyes filled again with tears of joy.

Flinging herself onto his lap and thence into his arms, she looked straight at him and answered from the heart, "Yes, Roberto, I will marry you. I'll follow you anywhere . . . if only you love me. That's all I ask . . ." Her voice trailed off as her lips sought his in formal acceptance of his proposal.

The sun dress she had put on for her return trip had crept well up onto her thighs as she had moved closer to Roberto. Now, as they kissed, his hand caressed the skin of her thigh, moving up under her hem to skim her hips and stomach. The flames of passion had been lit within them both. Eva moaned as she sought to deepen the kiss, her hands fiercely exploring the strong sinewy shoulders that loomed above her. They were both breathless when Roberto finally withdrew his hand and pried her from him.

"You're not making this any easier, sweetheart. We have plans to make, you know," he chided her, kissing a patch of auburn curls as he did so. He continued, "How soon can we be married—observing all proprieties, that is? This union is too precious to be clouded in any way."

Knowing exactly to what he referred, Eva imagined the reactions of those people—namely Stuart's family and friends, whom she disliked so—when she announced that she would be remarrying. Would she have to cater to their wishes in the future as she had to in the past? She burst out in alarm, "I don't care about proprieties, Roberto. We can't wait any six months or a year. I don't care what they say . . . they've already hurt me too much. I want you now, Roberto!" So desperate was her plea that he had to bury her head in his chest to avoid taking her there and then. As he stroked her hair, he spoke with conviction.

"This is what we'll do. I want you to come with me to São Paulo from here. We can spend a week or so there. I'll show you the sights, the best of which is the old mansion that is going to be your home." At the subtle reference to old mansions, which he knew Eva loved, she tilted her head up to exchange a smile of mutual understanding with him. He wasn't through with the itinerary, though.

"Then we'll fly with Paul back to Boston. You'd enjoy seeing his campus and I'd like you to meet my mother." He tightened his grip on her, a tender assurance of his support.

"I'd really like that. Will she like me?" she wondered aloud.

"She'll have to . . . a fellow American! Seriously, she'll love you. You're like her in many ways. And she's never had a daughter-in-law before!" He tickled her gently into easy laughter.

But Eva was becoming impatient. "Then what, Roberto? I haven't heard anything about a wedding yet. Are you getting cold feet already?"

"Patience, sweetheart! After Boston, we'll return here, to Terra Vermelho, for a very private little marriage ceremony. We really should wait longer, but I don't think there would be enough cold water for the both of us. At any rate, we can wait for a reasonable amount of time before announcing the marriage in the States, so people will merely think you're on an extended rest cure. How does it sound?" His eyes opened wide in anticipation of her reaction.

Eva's bubbled with excitement, though she teased him. "I don't know . . . several weeks is an awfully long time. I'm not sure I can restrain myself that long," she added, biting his ear playfully.

"You little minx," Roberto's voice came low and huskily, as he bodily lifted her and laid her on the bed. As he lowered himself over her, she raised her hands to his silver-winged sideburns, tracing their descent down his cheek.

"I've wanted to do that so many times," she whispered, her fingers now tracing the outline of his mouth in adoration.

"What I've wanted to do so many times would be improper just yet . . ." he growled mischievously.

Eva whispered then, for his ears alone, "Are you going to tell someone?"

His dark eyes studied hers for a long moment, drinking in the love, the need, the sensuality she offered.

"Not I!" was his terse pledge, and then there were no more words, as Roberto declared his eternal love for Eva with the greatest reverence of all.

Love—the way you want it!

Candlelight Romances

Once you've tasted joy and passion, do you dare dream of

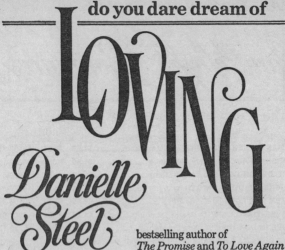

LOVING

Danielle Steel

bestselling author of
The Promise and *To Love Again*

Bettina Daniels lived in a gilded world—pampered, adored, adoring. She had youth, beauty and a glamorous life that circled the globe—everything her father's love, fame and money could buy. Suddenly, Justin Daniels was gone. Bettina stood alone before a mountain of debts and a world of strangers—men who promised her many things, who tempted her with words of love. But Bettina had to live her own life, seize her own dreams and take her own chances. But could she pay the bittersweet price?

A Dell Book ============================ **$2.75 (14684-4)**

Dell BESTSELLERS